1

BOOKS BY EDWARD DORN

POETRY

The Newly Fallen
Hands Up!
Geography
Idaho Out
North Atlantic Turbine
Twenty-Four Love Songs
Songs Set Two — A Short Count
Recollections of Gran Apacheria
Collected Poems
Manchester Square (with Jennifer Dorn)

PROSE

The Rites of Passage
    (Revised later as By the Sound)
Some Business Recently Transacted in the White
    World

NONFICTION

The Shoshoneans
    (with photographs by Leroy Lucas)

TRANSLATION
    (with Gordon Brotherston)

The Tree Between Two Walls
Our Word
Cesar Vallejo Selected Poems

SCREENPLAY

Abilene! Abilene!

Slinger

by Edward Dorn

Wingbow Press Berkeley 1975

GUNSLINGER is published by WINGBOW PRESS

Distributed by BOOKPEOPLE, 2940 Seventh Street, Berkeley, California 94710

First publication of the books here collected:
Gunslinger Book I, Black Sparrow Press, Los Angeles 1968
Gunslinger Book II, Black Sparrow Press, Los Angeles 1969
The Cycle, Frontier Press, West Newbury, Massachusetts 1971
Gunslinger Book III, Frontier Press, West Newbury, Massachusetts 1972

ISBN 0-914728-05-9 Trade Paper Edition
ISBN 0-914728-06-7 Trade Cloth Edition
ISBN 0-914728-07-5 Signed Cloth Edition

Library of CONGRESS Catalog Card No. 75-3658

BOOK
I

*The curtain might rise
anywhere on a single speaker*

for Paul Dorn

I met in Mesilla
The Cautious Gunslinger
of impeccable personal smoothness
and slender leather encased hands
folded casually
to make his knock.
He would show you his map.

There is your domain.
Is it the domicile it looks to be
or simply a retinal block
of seats in,
he will flip the phrase
the theater of impatience.

   If it is where you are,
the footstep in the flat above
in a foreign land

or any shimmer the city
sends you
the prompt sounds
of a metropolitan nearness
he will unroll the map of locations.

His knock resounds
inside its own smile, where?
I ask him is my heart.
Not this pump he answers
artificial already and bound
touching me
with his leathern finger
as the Queen of Hearts burns
from his gauntlet into my eyes.

    Flageolets of fire
he says there will be.
This is for your sadly missing heart
the girl you left
in *Juarez*, the blank
political days press her now
in the narrow adobe
confines of the river town
her dress is torn
by the misadventure of
        her gothic search

The mission bells are ringing
in Kansas.
Have you left something out:
Negative, says my Gunslinger,
no *thing* is omitted.

Time is more fundamental than space.
It is, indeed, the most pervasive
of all the categories
in other words
theres plenty of it.
And it stretches things themselves
until they blend into one,
so if youve seen one thing
youve seen them all.

I held the reins of his horse
while he went into the desert
to pee. *Yes,* he reflected
when he returned, that's less.

How long, he asked
have you been in this territory.

Years I said. Years.
Then you will know where we can have
a cold drink before sunset and then a bed
will be my desire
if you can find one for me
I have no wish to continue
my debate with men,
my mare lathers with tedium
her hooves are dry
Look they are covered with the alkali
of the enormous space
between here and formerly.
Need I repeat, we have come
without sleep from Nuevo Laredo.

And why do you have such a horse
Gunslinger? I asked. Don't move
he replied
the sun rests deliberately
on the rim of the sierra.

And where will you now I asked.
Five days northeast of here
depending of course on whether one's horse
is of iron or flesh
there is a city called Boston
and in that city there is ahotel
whose second floor has been let
to an inscrutable Texan named Hughes
Howard? I asked
The very same.
And what do you mean by inscrutable,
        oh Gunslinger?
I mean to say that He
has not been seen since 1833.

But when you have found him my Gunslinger
what will you do, oh what will you do?
You would not know
that the souls of old Texans
are in jeopardy in a way not common
to other men, my singular friend.

You would not know
of the long plains night
where they carry on
and arrange their genetic duels
with men of other states —

so there is a longhorn bull half mad
half deity
who awaits an account from me
back of the sun you nearly disturbed
just then.
Lets have that drink.
STRUM

strum

And by that sound
we had come there, false fronts
my Gunslinger said make
the people mortal
and give their business
an inward cast. They cause culture.
Honk HONK, Honk HONK Honk
that sound comes
at the end of the dusty street,
where we meet the gaudy Madam
of that very cabaret going in
where our drink is to be drunk —
        Hello there, Slinger! *Long time*
no see
what brings you, who's your friend,
to these parts, and where
if you don't mind my asking, Hello,
are you headed ..

Boston!? you don't say, Boston
is an actionable town they say
never been there myself
Not that I mean to slight the boys
but I've had some nice girls
from up Boston way
they turned out real spunky!

But you look like you
always did *Slinger, you*
still make me shake, I mean
why do you think I've got my hand on
my hip if not to steady *myself*
and the way I twirl this
Kansas City parasol
if not to keep the dazzle
of them spurs outa my eyes
Miss Lil! I intervened
you mustn't slap my
Gunslinger on the back
in such an off hand manner
I think the sun, the moon
and some of the stars are
kept in their tracks
by this Person's equilibrium
or at least I sense some effect
on the perigee and apogee of all
our movements in this, I can't quite say,
man's presence, the setting sun's
attention I would allude to
and the very appearance
of his neurasthenic mare
a genuine Nejdee
lathered, as you can see, with abstract fatigue

Shit, Slinger! you still got that
marvelous creature, and who *is this*
funny talker, you pick him up
in some sludgy seat of higher
learnin, Creeps! you always did
hang out with some curious refugees.

Anyway come up and see me
and bring your friend, anytime
if you're gonna be in town we
got an awful lot to talk about
for instance, remember that man
you was always looking for
name of Hughes?
Howard? I asked
You got it — that was
the gent's first handle
a texas dynamiter he was
back in '32
always turned my girls on a lot
when he blew In,
A man in the house
is worth 2 in the street
anyday, like I say this
Hughes *had a kind of interest*
about him, namely
a saddle bag full of currency
which don't hurt none
You remember there was this trick
they called her Jane —
she got religion & left the unit
but I heard this Hughes
Howard? I asked
Right, *boy*
they say he moved to Vegas
or bought Vegas *and*

                    moved it.
I can't remember which.
Anyway, I remember you had
what your friend here

might call an obsession
about the man —
don't tell me you're
still looking for him
I mean they say,
can't prove it by me,
this Hughes —
Howard? I asked
Hey Slinger you better shut
that boy up!
Cut it, my friend
I was just —
Drop it!
Anyway, they say
this Howard is kinda
peculiar about bein Seen
like anywhere anytime
sort of a special type
like a lotta texans I know
plumb strange the way
they operate.

You know,
I had to deal with a texan once
nearly drove one of my best girls Out,
insisted on her playing black jack
with his stud horse
who was pretty good
held the cards with his hooves
real articulate like and could add
fastern most humans
recall before I put a stop to it
we had special furniture
hauled in from Topeka.

That horse would sit at
the table all night, terrible
on whiskey and rolled
a fair smoke
and this texan insisted he was
payin for my girl's time
and he could use it any way he
saw fit
as long as he was payin like
and I had to explain
a technical point to that Shareholder
namely, that he was payin for her ass,
which is not time!

How did you get rid of him
I asked

Well boy, that was singular
you know I thought and thought
and I was plum stumpt
that is,
until one of my Regulars of the time
who had an interest in this girl
can't recall her name
but you'd know the fella
a wrangler from wyoming, THE Word
his name was
anyway he Suggested we
turn that horse on —
Hughes? I asked.
Jesus! Slinger can't you do
something about that refugee
no! his mother was Religious

so we turned this stud on
and it took most of a Tampico
shipment to do the job
but I'll tell you Slinger
that horse laughed all that night
and they carried him out next morning
and put him on the stage
for Amarillo, him and the texan
sittin in there all alone
and that horse was tellin everybody
what to do
Get that strong box up there,
get them "horses" hitched up
he'd say
rollin a big tampico bomber with his hooves
his shoes had come off, you see,
and he could do it so natural anyway
and then he'd kinda lounge
inside the stage coach and
lean out the window winkin
at the girls, showing
his teeth, I can't say he was
Unattractive, something kinda
handsome about his big face
and suggestive he was
a sorta manner
he had
    He kept sayin Can You Manage?
and Thank You!
every time the hostler hitched up
another horse
and then he had a kinda what
you might call a derisive air

when he'd say "Due In On Monday"
because you see it was Sunday
when they left town, but
he kept knockin his right hoof
against the inside of the coach
sayin You All Alright Out There?
and he had the texan's hat on
a stetson XX sorta cockwise
on his head it was
I tell you Slinger you would of
split your levis and dropped your
beads to seen it.

       Because he
was sayin some of the abstractest
things you ever heard
like Celery Is Crisp!
and we ain't seen him
or that individual texan
who owned him since.
I swear
that stud must have become a congressman
or something since then
He sure was going strong on that
fresh Tampico — Some of the hands
that was there that day in fact
claimed he didn't leave on the stage
at all, there's still people
around here who'll claim that horse
flew back west when the texan
went to sleep 5 miles out of town.

Where were we I asked,
when I noticed my Gunslinger
had retired to a shady spot
cast by the town's one cottonwood
Hold on, requested the Gunslinger
and held a conference to the side
with Lil

and then he kissed with a smile
her hand and she said *you boys*
enjoy yourself, I'll see about you later.

Then as we mounted the steps
of the cabaret
The Gunslinger sang

> *Oh a girl there was in the street*
> *the day we rode into La Cruz*
> *and the name of the name of her feet*
> *was the same as the name of the street*
> *and she stood and she stared like a moose*
> *and her hair was tangled and loose . . .*

STRUM
  strum

Do you know said the Gunslinger
as he held the yellow tequila up
in the waning light of the cabaret
that this liquid is the last
dwindling impulse of the sun
and then he turned and knelt
and faced that charred orb

as it rolled below the swinging doors
as if it were entering yet descending
and he said to me NO!
it is not. It is that
cruelly absolute sign my father
I am the son of the sun, we two
are always in search
of the third — who is that I asked
Hughes?
Howard?
Yes.
No.
Why not?
Because the third can never be
a texan
Never?
Yes.
Why not?
I told you, back there
when you held my horse.
Ah. If that is the case then
is your horse the Turned On
Horse of whom we've just now heard
and if that may be true how is it

your horse is also that
magnificently nervous mare
I've back there held?
Back There?
what is it you ask?

Is that your horse and was it
the Turned On Horse.
Possibly.

Possibly! what do you mean?
No, my horse is not a texan.
What?
Drink the yellow sun
of your tequila and calm
yourself, *Jack*
and then I shall tell you
because you are inattentive
and expect reason to Follow
as some future chain gang does
a well worn road.
Look, by the way, a fight
has started, order again
before the place is Smashed

      I then did order, yet
wondered, the inexplicability
of all that had, in this half
hour passed. And when
the divine tequilas were served
we two had retired to a table
obscure in the corner.

      Lo que pasa he breathed
this place is
in the constructive process
of ruin — Gaze upon it:
tables upended, the flak
of chips and drink surrounds us
with perfect, monday night slowmotion

And now my Gunslinger
in his steady way deliberated
on the scene before us — Note
he said
that confusion.
I did.
What do you see
he asked.
Men fighting I answered
Is that all, he asked
Do you want the deetails
I asked
Don't be evasive he replied
What is the *principle* of what
you see.
I was hard put to understand this
I tried.
The principle, I said
is leverage. Not quite
the Gunslinger rejoined,
that is the mechanism
I asked for the principle.
Yes you did, quite plainly
said I
But I am afraid I —
Never mind he said, are these
men men.
Yes I answered on the heated margin
of that general battle
Is my horse a horse? he continued
I'm on that score not sure
I said.

Your horse seemes different
from these men.
Quite right
but that's not altogether
what I am getting at.

                        Here
he said, passing me the cigarette.
I think, he added
of taking you to *L*as *V*egas.
Then you aren't going
to *B*oston. Not now he
exhaled, fresh distortions
as you yourself heard
have reached my ears.
Uh-huh I managed to exhale.

    Thus we sat and still
I knew not the principle
of which he spoke.

      STRUM

            strum

      Then there was an interlude
in which the brawl before our
indented eyes went on.

Auto-destruction he breathed
and I in that time was
suspended
as if in some margin of the sea
I saw the wading flanks
of horses spread in energy

What makes?
he suddenly asked in the smoke
and turmoil, and the bullets
flying,
What makes you think
oh what makes you
that this horse sitting between us
and who has not spoken
a word
or is it that I have
from the beginning
misjudged you.
The Horse grinned at me

Oh my Gunslinger, I said
If this be true
and it must be
because I can see in this horse
the Horse described
Will it not be very inappropriate
that Lil see this same Horse
in her establishment?
What of the girls?

Why, untaught alien
do you think I have arranged
this mass collision, standard in its design
you see raging not 15 feet away
but to distract the vision
of that spinning crystal?
She seemed nice enough to me
I said.
You have not lived 2000
and more years and as he
disengaged his eyes from mine
he said And speaking of said
Lady here, she, comes —

My god, Slinger, she said
I am at your service,
replied the Gunslinger.
Oh knock that off!
I've got a Business to tend to
and the smoke in this corner
is blindin besides, say
haven't I met that Horse
before? The Horse
rose from his chair and
tipped his stetson XX
Hello *L*il, it's been a long time
here have a seat,
we've got a lot to talk
about, *Slow down*
the Gunslinger said and
that was the only time
I ever heard anybody speak
obliquely to the Horse.

        Thus sat the four of us
at last a company it seemed
and the Bombed Horse took off his stetson
XX, and drew on the table
our future course.

Whispered, as I did, aside
to the Gunslinger, Who, finally,
is this gaudy Lil? Lil,
I didn't expect to see
here — we were in Smyrna
together, now called Izmir
when they burned the place
Down, we were
Very young then
I might add. Does that
satisfy you?
Yes I answered.

        And then
the Oblique Horse
having waited patiently
for the course of that aside
to run
asked Have you finished.
It occurred to me
I might not readily
Answer a Horse
but I was discouraged,
in whatever question
I might have felt,
when the Gunslinger
on my arm put

the pressure of his leatherbound
fingers and gave me
a look
in the aftermath of those bullets
and that dispersing smoke
which said, Quietly.

STRUM, strum

      Then sat we mid aftermath
and those unruly customers in Lil's
cabaret and the Plugged In Horse
covered the table
with his elaborate plans
and as he planned he rolled
immense bombers
from the endless Tampico
in his saddle bags.

What's happened to my black ace
the Horse inquired
scraping his chair, reaching
under the table,
smiling, passing at the same time
his bomber without limit to me.
But, I,
don't recognize
this size,
it is, beyond, me.
No, mortal, that size is beyond your conception
Smoke. Don't describe yourself.

That's right, referee, the Horse
thinks he's makin telescopes
Lil observed
but one often makes a remark
and only later sees how true it is!
Jast pass it! Hey Slinger!
Play some music.
Right, breathed the Gunslinger
and he looped toward the juke then,
in a trajectory of exquisite proportion
a half dollar which dropped home
as the .44 presented itself in the proximity
of his hand and interrogated the machine

A28, Joe Turner *Early in the Mornin'*
came out and lay on the turntable
His inquisitive .44 repeated the question
   and B13 clicked
Lightnin' Hopkins *Happy Blues for John Glenn,*
   and so on
the terse trajectories of silver then
the punctuations of his absolute .44
without even pushing his sombrero off his eyes

Gawddamit Slinger! there you go
wreckin my Wurlitzer again
sittin there
in that tipped back chair,
can't you go over to the machine
and put the money in and push
the button like a normal bein?
We're at the Very beginning of logic
around here

so them things cost money
and besides that *Slinger, some*
of these investors
is gettin edgy
since this Stoned Horse come in
they're talkin bout closin my place
Down
scarin my girls with hostyle talk.
My bartender gettin tighter
every time *you do some shit*
like that.
Don't bring me down Lil,
we'll be out of here by and by.

Yea Lil, drop it
the Stoned Horse said.
We'd all rather *be* there
than talk about it.
It's all right Lil, I
said. *Oh refugee*
you talk like a natural
mortal, take your hand
off my knee
I've got other things to do
now.

STRUM

Just then a Drifter carrying
a divine guitar
passed by our table and the guise

inlaid around the string cut hole
pulsated as do
stars in the ring
of a clear night
Hi! Digger
the drifting guitarist greeted
the Bombed Horse
who was in his saddle bags
rummaging
Heidigger? I asked
the Xtian Statistician
is that who you are?
Are you trying
to "describe" me, boy?
No, no, I hastened to add.
And by the way boy
if there's any addin
to do around here
I'll do it, that's my stick
comprende?
Where's my dark ace?

     Into the cord of that question
a stranger turned his brilliantined head
pulled open his fabrikoid coat
and Said
       What's your business
with Any dark ace!
               The scene
became a bas-relief
as the length of the bar froze
arms and legs, belts and buckles caught
drink stilled in mid-air

Yea! You! You're a horse
aincha? I mean you!
and, "looking around", *Horseface!*

                              strum

The Stoned Horse said Slowly
not looking up
from his rolling and planning
Stranger you got a *pliable lip*
you might get yourself described
if you stay on.

Come on!
Who's the horse, I mean who's
horse is that, we can't have
No Horse! in here.
It ain't proper
and I think I'm gonna
put a halter on you!

Uh uh, the Gunslinger breathed.
Anybody *know* the muthafucka
the Stoned Horse inquired
of the general air.
Hey, hear that the stranger gasped
that's even a *negra* horse!

Maybe so, maybe not
the Gunslinger inhaled
but stranger you got an Attitude
a mile long

as his chair dropped forward
all four legs on the floor
and as the disputational .44
occurred in his hand and spun there
in that warp of relativity one sees
in the backward turning spokes
of a buckboard,

             then came suddenly
to rest, the barrel utterly justified
with a line pointing
to the neighborhood of infinity.
The room froze harder.

Shit,
Slinger, Lil noticed, *You've pointed*
your .44 straight
out of town.
I keep tellin you
not to be so goddamn fancy
now that amacher's
got the drop on you!

    Not so, Lil!
the Slinger observed.
Your vulgarity is flawless
but you are the slave
of appearances —
this Stockholder will find
that his gun cannot speak
he'll find
that he has been Described

                                Strum

the greenhorn pulled
the trigger and his store-bought iron
coughed out some cheap powder,
and then changed its mind,
muttering about having
been up too late last night.
Its embarrassed handler
looked, one eye wandering,
into the barrel
and then reholstered it and
stood there.

strum

The total .44
recurred in the Slinger's hand
and spun there
then came home like a sharp knock
and the intruder was described —
a plain, unassorted white citizen.

You can go now,
the Turned On Horse said.
*That investor'd make
a good janitor* Lil observed,
*if I was gonna keep this place
I'd hire him.*

What does the foregoing mean?
I asked. Mean?
my Gunslinger laughed
Mean?

Questioner, you got some strange
obsessions, you want to know
what something *means* after you've
seen it, after you've *been* there
or were you *out* during
That time? No.
And you want some *reason*.
How fast are you
by the way? No local offense
asking that is there?
No.

        I like you mi nuevo amigo
for a mortal you're exceptional
How fast are you?
Oh, average fast I suppose
or maybe a little more
than average fast, I ventured.
Which means
you gotta draw.
Well, yes.
Umm, considered the Gunslinger
taking the telescope
from the Turned On Horse.

Please don't hold my shortcoming
against me oh Gunslinger
and may I enquire of you —
Enquire? he breathed
don't do *that*
Well then may I . . .
no I wouldn't do that Either

How is it then?
How can such speed be?
You make the air dark
with the beauty of your speed,
Gunslinger, the air
separates and reunites as if lightning
had cut past
leaving behind a simple experience.
How can such aching speed be.
Are you, further,
a God
or Semidiós
and therefore mortal?

      First things first
he reflected in the slit of his eyes
your attempt
is close
but let me warn you
never be close.
A mathematician from Casper Wyoming
years ago taught me That
To eliminate the draw
permits an unmatchable Speed
a syzygy which hangs tight
just back of the curtain
of the reality theater
down the street,
speed is not necessarily fast.
Bullets are not necessarily specific.
When the act is
so self contained
and so dazzling in itself

the target then
can disappear
in the heated tension
which is an area between here
and formerly
In some parts of the western world
men have mistakenly
called that phenomenology —

You mean, I encouraged
there is no difference
between appearance and —
"*R*eality?" he broke in
I never "mean", remember,
that's a *mortal* sin
and Difference I have no sense of.
That might be *your* sin
and additionally —
Don't *add*, that's my stick,
the Horse said smiling.
Furthermore, the Gunslinger instructed —
More is more divine
said the Immobile Horse
Furthermore, don't
attempt to burden me
with your encouragement
because
to go on to your second Question,
I am un semidiós.

And so you are mortal
after all said I

No mortal, you describe
yourself
I die, he said
which is not
the same as Mortality,
and which is why I move
between the Sun and you
the ridge is my home
and it's why you seem
constructed of questions, uh,
What's your name?

i, I answered.

That's a simple name
Is it an initial?
No it is a single.

strum

            Nevertheless,
it is dangerous to be named
and makes you mortal.
If you have a name
you can be sold
you can be told
by that name leave, or come
you become, in short
a reference, or if bad luck
is large in your future
you might become an institution
which you will then mistake

for defense. I could
now place you
in a column from which
There is No Escape
and down which The Machine
will always recognize you.
Or a bullet might be Inscribed
or I could build a maze
called a *social investigation*
and drop you in it
your name
into it —

Please! I implored him
you terrify me.
What then, I asked
is my case? looking into
the Odd toed ungulate's eyes
who had his left leg resting on my shoulder.
The mortal can be described
the Gunslinger finished,
That's all mortality is
in fact.

STRUM

    Are you hungry
mortal I
the Gunslinger asked
and Yes I answered reflecting.

Well then Lil,
let's have some food
of two sorts
before we depart for Vegas.
Lil snapped
her gaudy fingers
and drink was brought
but not for the Classical Horse
who forewent drink
with a brush of his articulate hoof.

The usual he said
Usual! There's nothin
usual about your diet Claude
Lil said, *Horse chestnuts with the*
spiny covering in tact
and 38 stalks of celery
in a large bowl.
Claude I enquired —
Don't enquire boy
It can be unhealthy
pass the salt
Do you get called Claude?
Why not? Listen, I,
I'm as mortal as you
born in santa fe
of a famous dike
who spelled it
with an e too.
So your name is *not*
Heidegger after all, then
what is it? I asked.
Lévi-Strauss.

Lévi-Strauss?
Do I look like his spouse!

No . . . I mean I've never
seen his wife.
You're a very observant type
Claude replied.
Well what do you do I persisted.
Don't persist.
I study the savage mind.
And what is that I asked.
That, intoned Claude leaning on my shoulder
is what you *have*
in other words, you provide
an instance
you are purely animal
sometimes purely plant
but mostly you're just a
classification, I mean it's conceivable
but so many documents
would have to be gone through
and dimensions of such *variety*
taken into account to realize what
you are, that
even if we confined ourselves
to the societies for which
the data are sufficiently full,
accurate, and comparable
among themselves
it could not be "done"
without the aid of machines.

Got it! the Slinger asked
Yea, I *heard* it I said
Not the same thing he said
Tell me more I said
The Horse has an interest in business,
haven't you noticed.
Noticed? I replied
Forget it he said, remember
you're just average fast.
The Horse is a double agent —

strum

Oh? But what about his name
Claude Lévi-Strauss is that —
Yes, you guessed it
a homonym. Don't get bugged Amigo

strum

Here comes Lil.
OK, the Gunslinger breathed
we're briefed
Hughes? I asked
Not now the Slinger said
here's Lil
Slinger! that Drifter claims
he can sing you a song.
What shimmering guesswork
the Slinger smiled
and beckoned to the young guitarist.

strum

      As he travels across
the cabaret may I ask
a question? Move on he said.
Are those rounds
in the .44
of your own making?
No bullets, I rarely use
ordinary ammunition.
What then?
Straight Information.
What?
You sound like the impact of a wet syllojsm

Look, into each chamber
goes one bit of my repertoire
of pure information,
into each gesture, what
you call in your innocence
"the draw"
goes Some Dark Combination
and that
shocks
the eye-sockets of my detainers
registers what my enemies
can never quite recall.

      Another question.
Naturally.
What do you know
of Love?
Know? Nada, if I knew it
it couldn't be Love.
Even a mortal knows that.

Then, what *is* it?
IS is not the link
it takes nine hundred years
to explain one blown
spark of Love
and you don't have
that much time Amigo.
How can you?
Leave it friend
I was with Gladys,
in Egypt
witnessed messengers
turned into phantoms.

He pressed one long finger between
his eyes —
it beats me how you mortals
can think something *is*.
Hush, pues, here comes our Drifta.

STRUM

Salud, poeta
what song can you sing?
All songs but one.
A careful reply.
Then can you sing
a song of a woman
accompanied by that
your lute which this
company took to be a guitar
in their inattention.

Yes I can, but
an *Absolute* I have
here in my hand.
Ah yes, the Gunslinger exhaled
It's been a long time.

    The drifting singer
put one foot on a chair
and began

I shall begin he said

    the Song about a woman

    On a plane of this plain
ſtood a dark colonnade
which cast its black shadows
in the form of a conception made
where I first saw your love
her elbows at angles

    her elbows at black angles

    her mouth
a disturbed tanager, and
in her hand an empty damajuana,
on her arm an emotion
on her ankle a band
a slender ampersand

    her accent so superb
she spoke without saying
and within her eyes
were a variety
of sparkling moments

Her thighs were monuments
of worked flesh
turned precisely to crush
what they will enclose
and in her manner is a hush

as if she shall enrage
with desire
with new fire
those maddened to taste
from her jewelled toes
to her swelled black mound
her startled faun

which has the earthy smell
of slightly gone
wild violets

O Fucking Infinity! O sharp organic thrust!
the Gunslinger gasped
                    and his fingers
spread across the evening atmosphere
My Sun tells me we have approached
the 24th hour
Oh wake the Horse!

    Lil, will you join us
on our circuit to Vegas?
Leave this place and be done?
The stage sits at the post
its six abnormal horses driverless,
chafing their bits
their corded necks are arching
toward the journey

How far is it Claude?

                    Across
two states
of mind, saith the Horse.
But from Mesilla said I
to Las Vegas — Vegas!
the Horse corrected
have you been asleep
. . . Must be more like
a thousand miles.
More like? he laughed
as we waited
for the Slinger
on his long knees
facing the burning hoop
as it rolled under
the swinging doors west

Mortal what do you mean
asked the Horse lounging and yawning
More Like!
how can distance
be more like.

        Thus, in the thickening vibration
our departure took shape
and Lil
the singer holding her arm
followed us out the swinging doors
and into the stage coach we got
and the Horse was leaning out
making his pitch

distributing fake phone numbers
and baring his teeth and the singer
was whispering a lyric to Lil
who had her hand on the Slinger's knee
and he was looking at me

And the stage its taut doubletree
transfixed and luminous shot forth
and the Horse
pulling from his pocket
his dark glasses
put them on and spoke not
and by those five missionaries
Mesilla was utterly forgot.

BOOK
II

for Jennifer

This tapestry moves
as the morning lights up.
And they who are in it move
and love its moving
from sleep to Idea
born on the breathing
of a distant harmonium, To See
is their desire
as they wander estranged
through the lanes of the Tenders
of Objects
who implore this existence
for a plan and dance wideyed
provided with a schedule
of separated events
along the selvedge of time.

Time does not consent.
This is morning
This is afternoon
This is evening
Only celebrations concur
and we concur To See
                    The Universe

All may wake who live
the combination is given
and Some comb the connections
in blind search
there are deaths at birth
there is death at 21
            and burial at 80
each calculation
involves another century.

Our company thus moves collectively
along the River Rio Grande.

The poet starts the strings,
as sleep inhabits the stage,
along the silver of a morning raga,
So this raga disperses
as the shimmering of its sense goes out,
Into the dry brilliance of the desert morning
Along the vanes of the willow leaves
Along the hallucination of the atmospheric realism
Into the upper reaches of the Yggdrasillic yoga
Over inner structure of the Human Thing
like Unto the formation of the pinnate ash
in which our treehouse sways

and the samara goes wingèd, Oh wild Angelica!
Oh quickbeam! oh quake and sway into waking,
With aspergill enter Into the future

        Suddenly the doubled reflection
of a distant butte
appear in the Slingers opened eyes
He speaks the word Whitehare
and makes a wish
for the 1st day of the month and then chants
Have you noticed how everboring
the following day is,
If there be nothing new but that which is

And then he stretched
so that, sitting between the Horse
and Lil, his limbs pierced the windows
on both sides
and the stage had arms.
How like a winter hath my absence been
observed the Slinger to himself
yet unable to stifle his yawn
for his hands were with his arms
off stage.

        Aah . . . In the high west
there burns a furious Starre
It is morning

Poet, that raga is called
The Coast of the Firmament

Then you know it?

Perfectly

I dont think the Perfect
can be known.

Very good. Then you must
never consort with the Perfect,
stick to the Absolute, it's
pliable, and upon it
you seem to play any tune
you choose. Can we have
a morning song? now.
Yet first, do you sing the traditional Rock
Oh Light; The Light!

    Then, as the poet
fixed his 'Lute
the Slinger parted the curtains
to have a look at the stereoscopic world.
From your sweet voice
I am astoned,
before you begin, he said
as the poet began,

        Now; get this action right!
        When I say light I mean the light
        Thats the light within the light
        Thats the mornin thats the light
        Light the mornin light the light
        Thats the natchral thats all right
        Oh baby, light the morning like the light

Oh baby, light the morning like the night
Put the mornin where it's tight

Hey theres the sun hes comin in
Theres the bird shes back again
Make the sun hes comin up
Make the bird shes gonna sing
Turn your head, dig let it *rang*

Oh baby douse the funky night
Put the mornin where it's tight.

A roll of Solar Reality,
my friend, your mind
is marvelously heliocentric
your fingers have been brushed
by the fleece on Aries flank.

Thus
I see we are yet some distance
outside Universe City, will you please
then, draw your fingers
across a variation of the line
"Cool Liquid Comes"
so that the roots of my soul
may be loosened and grow past
the hardness of the Future.

The poet turned the claws
of the Golden Griffin
of his pure lute
and absolved the strings.
I hope I can make that he breathed.

Cool Liquid Comes
he whispered
and grazed an ascension
of notes, he sang

    Cool liquid comes
    the morning . . . sensing . . .
    the morning sensing Inne
    the blend of spatial hours
    cool blending comes

    Comes blending the arc
    comes gripping urge timing
    the κυκλος blanching
                the plain

    branding morning
    on the worlds side
    the great plaining zodiacus
    The great brand of our crossing
    the fabulous accounting
    of our coursing
    the country of our consciousness

    Cool comes the greatness
    the scalar beauty intointoo
    oh our morning bright environment
    along the passage of our company
    into the hoodoos
    lying around the foot of our future

Cool flight along our trail
comes a rupture of feathers,
Laterally comes the desert lark
throat of memory of an extinct tree
into the light of afterdark
gone out to the dry sea in bateaux

Cool dry,
Shall come the results of inquiry
out of the larks throat
oh people of the coming stage
out of the larks throat
loom the hoodoos
beyond the canyon country
Oh temptation of survival
oh lusterless hope
of victory in opposites

Cool Liquid, cool liquid distilled
of the scalar astral spirit
morning sensing congealing
our way, hours of spatial cooling
weighing the lark appealing

Oh Narrowness of protestation!

And oh in the cool lateral morning even
in the cool wide burn of
our œnanthic unrest and willfullness
we move west and no more
Shall Dawn Bless our Altar Cloth

Aye singer. O absolutist.
You have sung a spelling account
of this Zone, yet
what a way to begin the morning!
Aye, Aye, you have lyricd
somewhat predestinarian
as all things of the imagination
must be. Thank you nomad,
for that rendering
of the Panorama.

    The singer took away
the yellow rose
from his pleated blousecuff
and presented it
to the morning wind
then turned to adjust his astrolabe
and applied the oil of Atropine
to its working parts.
Andromeda turns and flashs
on the far shore, he observed.

The Slinger crossed his sheathèd legs
and pulling on his vest
fastened the mescal buttons
thereon and truly turned his eyes
into the landscape, Who
is this? he asked.

Is that an abstract question?

No, it seems material
but we'll know more
if the horses choose to stop.

What can you see then
with the sun on our right
in this vacuum of social infinity
that you blink your eyes so?
asked the poet

When most I wink then do mine eyes best see.
A man appears. He gestures
with his thumb. The six driverless horses
are inquisitive, they draw to a stop.

Wayfarer,
Have you a name
for Fate to use
when she pulls the end of your time
off the spool?

Yes. A birth Pang
from my mothers mind

A diacritical remark,
What is it?

Kool Everything.

    We Did!
several miles back
awoke and spoke the Horse
yawning thru the awning.)

Your surname I find hard
to place, its *generalness*
is overwhelming.

My fathers seed burst away
as the autumn dispersal
of a milkweed pod
conveying me into my mothers womb
via the wind.

A windy beginning!
What is the name of your throat?

Huh!?

You have introduced your thumb
yet omitted his name

Man I dont know where youre At
I'm just hitchhiking
to Universe City and beyond
Where you going?

Universe City.

Can I have a ride?

That was assumed gesturelessly
the six driverless horses
stop only to pick up.
What keeps you beside the road?

Dispersal, friend
my Head has been misplaced.

Then climb in
and get yourself centered
we approach the outskirts.

Our company moves once more
in the swift running coach
across the sparkling morning
thru the sharp rising scent
of the sage scattered river hills.

And in the Yellow Rose of Dawn
Miss Lil reads her encyclopædia
in a slender handled mirror
held before her
in her exquisitely strung hand
and reaffirms
that ancient arrangement of amaranthine flesh
the quick aniline of flawless brow
the pure full readyness of her lips
the open public amazement of her silken cheek,
And I shall turn, into a Bluebird
she sings to the breeze and then
with some Smiles she arrives at the dock
in a Masserati and boards the ship of Dawn.

Smoke? asked Everything
offering the lady his jewel◈studded bag.

What is it?

Tobacco.

No thank you. What's your name.

Kool Everything.

You better stay away from tobacco
or you might do just that, Pardner.

What happened to I she asked
his eyes dont seem right.

I is dead, the poet said.

That aint grammatical, Poet.

Maybe. However Certain it seems,
look, theres no reaction.

Shake him no more then!
requested the Gunslinger,
we'll keep him with us
for a past reference
Thus are his cheeks the map of days outworn,
Having plowed the ground
I has turned at the end of the row
a truly inherent *versus*
.daeha sa kcab emas eht si I ecnis

Thus this poor individual
likc all the singulars of his race
came in forward and goes out sternward
and some distant starre flashes even him
an indiscriminate salute.

That sounds deep, Slinger
But it makes me sad
to see I go, he was,
I mean I was so perplexed
I's obsessions were almost real
me and I had an understanding
I dont like to see I die.

I dont wish to distract you
with the metaphysics of the situation Lil
yet be assured,
I aint dead.

I know *that, Slinger.*
It's possible you missed it
the Slinger allowed,
I speak of *I*
Him? Lil pointed.
Is that not I? Stilled
inside whoever he is.
Oh. Well I'll be . . .
We never knew anything much
about him did we. I
was the name he answered to,
and that was what he had
wanderin around inside him
askin so many questions
his eyes had already answered
But wheres he at
If I aint dead?

    Life and Death
are attributes of the Soul
not of things. The Ego
is costumed as the road manager
of the soul, every time
the soul plays a date in another town
I goes ahead to set up
the bleechers, or book the hall
as they now have it,
the phenomenon is reported by the phrase

I got there ahead of myself
I got there ahead of my I
is the fact
which not a few anxious mortals
misread as intuition. The Tibetans
have a treatise on that subjeftion.
Yet the sad fact is I is
part of the thing
and can never leave it.
This alone constitutes
the reality of ghosts.
Therefore I is not dead.

Imagine that, Lil said
patting I's stiff knee.

We wont have to Everything offered
it's gonna be hot soon.
I only mean I never met I
but if he turns out to be put together
like most people I's gonna
come apart in the heat.
You see what I mean?

The boy has a point Slinger
it could get close fast in here.

    Yes, reflected the Poet
As the Yellow Rose of Dawn climbs
he loses the light azimuthal fragrance of his arrival
and becomes a zenith
of aparticular attention —
All Systems Go.

There will be some along our way
to claim I ſtinks.

The Slinger considered this
conference of voices
yet could relate very little
to the realness
of the engendering emergency.
Since I am extraTerrestial he said
I have no practical sense of smell.

        More likely you can't keep your nose
out of those $50 bags,
observed the Horse. Anyway
we can drop it off at a bus stop
as we go thru Albuquerque
that populationll never know the difference.

I would urge you, friends.
I is a reference to the past
and cannot be So dropped
If I stinks, it is only thus
we shall not so easily forget
his hour of darkness.

        Perhaps the Slinger signals a detour
past a probable and dangerous lapse
counseled the Singer. By the way
Everything, what Have you
in that 5 gallon gas can?

Huh!? oh that.
well thats, uh,
Acid.

How pure is it?

Straight man.
1000 percent,
nothin but molecules.

Will you pour a little on this
and the Poet took away from his blousecuff
the Supreme Colorless Rose
of Noon
and held it under the spout.

Thank you, Kool.
The poet then presented
the Rose to his nose
and sniffed the autotheistic chemical
What subtle richness he whispered
this would turn one into an allegory
and after an inordinately long time
he observed all eyes upon him
and said I believe,
not that it matters,
this to be our solution
the perceptual index
of Everythings batch
is High, to say the least.
What then, if we make I
a receptable of what
Everything has,
our gain will be twofold,
we will have the thing
we wish to keep
as the container of the solution
we wish to hold

a gauge in other words
in the form of man.
It is a derangement of considerable antiquity.

Instead of formaldehyde?
Lil asked

Exactly, replied the poet.

What will that do to I
and what will it do
to my uncut batch
Everything wondered.

Only Time can reveal the immaterial
the poet said, rolling up
I's sleeve, at the same time
hanging the 5 gallon can spout down
from the ceiling of the coach
and adjusting the tubes.

I wont hold 5 gallons
Everything said as tho
he'd thot of a hitch.

I will the poet answered
we'll use his stomach too,
and elaborated,
All that I will hold
we will put into him.

That, observed the Slinger
is where your race
put its money.

Advice is common, answered the poet
the race is not over.

Well said, breathed the Slinger.

    We're inside
the outskirts, announced the Horse,
a creature of grass and only marginally
attracted to other distortions.
Here we are in the sheds
and huts of the suburbs. There are
some rigid types in here.
It's kinda poignant
but that doesnt move it any closer to the center.

Yup! empty now of all but a few
stubborn housewives
and disturbed only by the return
of several husbands known to be unable
to stay away during this celestial repast
called lunch. Thats where youre out
before you leave. Theres a man
turning on his sprinkler, it should be illegal
a small spray to maintain his grass, the Edible
variety no one doubts.
But I see none of my friends grazing there
these green plots
must be distress signals to God
that he might notice
their support of one of his minor proposals
He must be taken by these remote citizens
to be the Patron of Grass.

Holy shit, *L*awn grass . . .
from that great tribe
they selected something to *M*ow

And the Horse came apart laughing
pounding his belly so that the coach swayed
and rocked from the shifting about
of his 14 hundred pounds.

      Hey Horse!
youre gonna loosen all the connections!
youre gonna spill the cargo!

Dont lower the Horse,
Gunslinger admonished Everything
He has a pure Head.
It's a rare thing these days. *And*
Our mission is to encourage the Purity of the Head
pray we dont lose track of our goal.

Sorry Horse, Kool said gently
I lost my head.

Forget it Everything, youve got
a lot on your mind. Here, have a chew
off my plug.

Is that Tennessee roughcut?

No, it's Pakistani Black.

Thanks. It exudes the sweat of young boys.

I wouldnt appreciate that.
The Slingers right I guess, I am
a pure head. Here, let me help you
with those tubes.

No, No, thats *ok*
it's kinda delicate work.

And when, the grass comes u-up
sang the Horse

> And when the grass goes dow-own
> And when, the fair yong sor-rel
> lies in the green green tow-own
> the para-dice will floo-rish
> And we'll be moving gra-zing
> in the wind, oh in-to the oowind.
> And when, the grass comes u-up
> and *when* the wind goes dow-own
> We'll *Flash* on our own legs then
> and nev-er-more come dow-own

An Equestrial song Horse,
I'm moved next to your race by its beauty,
the poet related with a look of sadness,
I hope you make it.

The Gunslingers eyes were covered
with his slender fingers.
*I'm al*right Lil whispered
when the hand of Everything
touched her shoulder, *I'm*
just *looking for my handkerchief.*

There was the faintest semblance
of a smile on I's posthumous mouth.

   The Poet took away
from his embroidered lapel
the Rose of High Noon
too intense to be seen
too bright to be identified by color
and with a sigh of regret
presented it to the rising thermal dust
where it became inset
in the scrolls of the precious atmosphere.

   We're *Here!* laughed Everything

Sounds like an adverb
disguised as a place, commented the Slinger

What?

Sounds like an adventure.

Oh, yea, man I *never thot* I'd see this place.

Then you'll have the privilege of seeing it
without having thot it, prompted the Slinger.

Let's have Lunch, said Lil,
I'm starved.

Then youre beyond the hand of Lunch
diagnosed the Slinger

Scheduled food is invariably tasteless
said the Poet.

Yet in the desert
you'd be happy to eat the schedule itself
the Slinger finished.

  And so, they all decoached
in Old Town. And having touched
their soles to terra firma
they all stood deeply and fully struck
and their physical peripheries grew so dumb
that they appeared studiously normal
when I decoached unaided
and attended only by an attitude
of such expressive conception
he seemed the offspring of a thousand laboratories.

I has shot past mortification
whispered the Slinger

I carries the Broken Code
the key to proprioception,
is it possible he has become the pure Come
of become, asked the Poet
of the Slinger's ear.

Would you put that into my ear
another way?

Por nada.
I is now an organ Ization
a pure containment

He has become a Five, Gallon, Can
I is now a living Batch

Me heard you the First time
the Slinger nodded
thats a Very interesting tautology.

    The Tautology walked
from the stage step to the hitching post
and there stroked the manes
of the six driverless horses, latherbathed and steaming.

Thats never before been done, Slinger breathed

Whats happening to my batch, Kool enquired

Your batch is now The batch
expropriation is accomplished
we stand before an original moment
in ontological history, the self, with one grab
has aquired a capital S, mark the date
the Gunslinger instructed,
we'll send a telegram to Parmenides.

That shits not gonna help me, Kool exploded
I was going to retire on that batch!

I has, the Slinger corrected,
at which Everything fell to the ground.

    Our company reassembled itself
and followed I with a triple impression —

for now they sought
to keep track of what they Had,
invested in where it Was,
and carried by where it's At

We need help, the Poet reckoned.

   A band of citizens gathered.
They blocked the way. They too
were meshed with the appearance of I
Tho their interest was inessentially
soldered to the surface, and tho
they had nought invested, an old appetite
for the Destruction of the Strange
governed the massed impulse of their tongues
for they could never comprehend
what the container contained.
Whats That! they shouted
Why are his eyes turned north?
Why are his pants short on one side?
Why does his hair point south?
Why do his knees laugh?
How does his hat stay on?
Wherez his ears?
The Feathers around his ankle!
What does his belt buckle say,
What do his shoes say,
we cant hear them!
Why dont his socks agree!
Theres a truckpatch in his belly button
does he have a desire to grow turnips?!
He hasnt bought a license for his armpits!

Look! they shouted,
his *name* is missing
from his shirt pocket
and his Managers name
is missing from his back,
He must be a Monster! Look
His pocket meters show Red
and they all laughed and screamed
This Vagrant, they shouted,
has got *nothing*, has no *cash*
and *no card*, he hasn't got a *Pot* . . .

Into the dead center of this ellipsis
the Slinger shot a complex gesture
and his mouth worked feverishly
thru the data of a forgotten alphabet
and his eye tracked smoothly toward the East
and there was produced in I's right hand
a Pot, and in his left hand *a Window*
exactly between the citizens voices
. . . to piss in or a w i n d o w
like when the Plug is pulled.

    Whereupon the Slinger
with a bow of *great* elaboration
and Immense profundity
turned to the half hyphen crazed crowd and said
I thank you, kind people,
for your lunchtime welcome,
you have greeted us with a kiwanis enthusiasm
we have been welcomed by Lions
as the sign outside your town predicted.

Witchcraft! shouted a man deep inside the crowd
and was instantly conveyed to within one inch
of the Slingers nose
by an arm become a boom, its fingers
encircling the mans neck — You are correct
citizen, your identification is the *same*
as your word for fear!

Huh?! Put me down!

Whereupon the Slinger opened his fingers,
and the citizen dropped into the dust.

  So this is Universe City
Lil annotated.

So it is, echoed Everything.
Used to be called Truth or Consequences
they ordered the truth
and got shipped the consequences
One of their mainstreet thinkers
must have thot they could make it back
with something Large — thats how come
it looks like a rundown movie lot
a population waiting around to become
White Extras. Wide spots in the road
have a tendency to get wider
due to the weight and speed
of the traffic going thruem.

Isnt that Interesting
Lil thot
as if she were not listening.

        Everything tugged
at the Slingers embroidered sleeve
Hey, now that you dealt the crowd
why dont we have a walk around the plaza
stretch our legs, pan the scene

you know, get it Right,
we dont wanna go straight into an automatic scarf
Let's exercise — shoot some grass.

You have an impeccable sense
of everything, including
the next step, the Slinger had to say.

Yeah, well thats because
I think I saw Dick Tracy
descend in a bucket with crutches.

Is that an alarm?

No brother it's a fact.
Now he's walkin toward us
trying to get on the soundtrack
of a flick titled Reality
but look! some wit stamped Crime Watcher
on his forehead when he wasnt lookin
Let's move!

Hang light, Kool,
the earth moves beneath your feet
like a ball bearing.

    The travelers drift easily
around the plaza, I
examines the jewellery of the native women

with the rhythmic patience of Eternity.
He gradually drops behind.

The poet accompanies Lil
and guides her meanderings
over the civilian and pseudo-historic terrain
as if he had spent late hours
pouring over charts.

    The Horse evangelizes
now and again
the reinchecked horses
of the plaza, bringing news
beyond the heads of most of them. Still,
One big white runs off immediately
when it is explained to her the reins
are not fixed to the ground,
and into the ear of a tall black
standing in front of the saloon
the message ran straight and clear.

    This horse laughed out loud
and tore the finely tooled saddle
off his back by hooking the belly strap
on a knot in the hitching rail
whereupon he seized the pommel
with his Great Teeth and pitched
the whole affair thru the swinging doors
leaving one of them banging
off one hinge. A loud
vacuum of pure silence
flowed suddenly forth
from that busy place.

        And in its wake,
with a punctuality almost
beyond relief, appeared the Owner
of the saddle
and the horse
guns in both hands
cigar between teeth
hat on head sideways
his face a miracle of undocumented
attention, his eyes
engaged in full count down
his head is a spasm
of presyntactic metalinguistic urgency

What What What
Where Where Where
Who What Where
What Where Who

        Someone conducts a search
for simple social data
a quest abstracter than Parsifals
the Slinger commented
as his group strolled past the scene.

I dont think so the stoned Horse said
This owner seeks a χίμαιρα

What a difficult target to find
The Slinger smiled
I havent seen one since December

And thats gone north for the Winter
the Horse reckoned

Immediately these words
out of the Horses mouth were out
the enraged Owner discharged
ten rounds with such ferocious rapidity
the bullets got stuck back to front
crowding each other out of the barrel
and fell to the boardwalk
as two segmented slugs 12345
each about 2½ inches in length.
Plunk Plunk said Kool Everything
and picked up one of the formations
and handed it to the Slinger who spoke on it

Brilliant. I'm sure Ive never seen
the result of such ferocity, a stutter
of some deep somatic conflict, this owner
was ill-advised to use a gun at all
and least of all to let it speak for him.

You see, he continued
turning to Lil and the Poet
this can only be
materialism, the result
of merely *real* speed. All
the smoothest gunnies Ive known
were metaphysicians and of course
no jammonings of this sort
were ever associated with their efforts
and the slug was then handed to the poet.

A timejam of some crudeness
observed the poet, the bullets are dead
lead has been rendered to lead.

Yes, lead is a Heavy metal
the Slinger agreed, Whats that Crunch?
Everything asked and the group
turned in time to see
the Owners gun fall to pieces
in his terrifik Hamlike grip, the pearl
powdered, the ferrament altogether crushed
at the same the Owners hulk
settled into a sort of permanence
as if a ship, gone to the bottom
shifts several ways into the sand
while finding her millennial restingplace.

It has become an Old Rugged Statue
of the good ol days, Everything gasped
a summary of accounts compiled
from frontier newspapers,
it must be worth a pile do you think
we should auction it? On the spot
answered the Horse who had a gavel
and began to pound upon a barrel
Do I hear a dollar, and he heard a dollar
and since money speaks the company left him
at the direction of a lively scene.

Kool Everything promenaded
with the Slinger and bent his ear
toward a piece of Explanation picked up
from an hand bill he found
on the ground where the stage stopped

This kinda talkie sounds new.
It's a revolutionary medium
It's sure to turn everything around.

Sounds as tho it's meant only for you
commented the Slinger

Thats the trouble with a name like mine
What I mean is Everybody —
A tangible change, the Slinger noticed.

Everybodys *got* to see this

Is all the world a cinema then?

Name this thing.

Well, There's a *Literate Projector*,
which, when a 35 mm strip is put thru it
turns it into a Script
Instantaneously!
and projects that — the finished script
onto the white virgin screen
and theyre gonna run it
in Universe City tonight

Is there no more
to this Reversal asked the Slinger.

Yea,
it will Invent a whole new literachure
which was Already There
a lot of big novels will get restored
in fact Everything, uh, I mean
all of it can be run the other way —
some of the technikalities
havent been worked out for documentaries
but let's face it,

you could rerun I mean all of it
¡atención! — Shoot a volcano, project it
and See the Idea behind it
sit down at the geologic conference
and hear the reasons Why
skip the rumble, move into the inference.
Eventually you could work your way back
to where it's still really dark
all the way back of the Brain?!

Hows it powered?

2 hundred and 40 shots
into the same instant
any outlet.

Every outlet?

No, just any.
Theres no color of course
It's gonna be a black and white script
even when it's a color film,
you see, parrots dont show up

Hows that?

Well, I'm not sure, handbill dont say.
But colors kinda complex, probly can't
uncrank intime to send it the other way
it's got something to do with reality
comprende, Bwana?

Forever, inhaled the Slinger

See! theres the marquee.━━━━━━➣

Literate Projector

And get this
They can distort the Projector
so that the script Departs
from the film, in Front!
now brother
thats complex, every day is payday
like April 1st!

There is but one Logos
tho many Images audition
the Slinger intervened.

What?!

Resume your Ontology, Everything.

Ontology? I'm just
telling you a story
about this projector, thats all.

My medium friend, nothing
which is demonstrative, as
this L.P. seems to be,
is ever All, for one thing
it is locked on this Side
of the Beginning, Toward what
are you pointing by so speaking
of the projector as the Sunne
and the Script as Holy Writ?

Fantasía, in other images
this machine makes it possible
for people who can't make films
to produce scripts and,
as the author of the handbill
is at some pains to point out
it was designed for the Stix
but works best in University towns
and other natural centers of doubletalk.
To put it in another Can
the Literate Projector
enables the user to fail insignificantly
and at the same time show up
behind a vocabulary of How It Is
Shake a circus up and down
put funny music next to Death
Or document something
about military committment
and let woodchucks play the parts
so say something quick about the war
in, well you know where the War is.

The point is it has to be read
to be seen, and like if the accent
is so incomprehensible and hysterical
it can only be coming from inside
the cinerama of the 3rd Reich
youre just not supposed to hear it.

Like as the waves make toward the Pebbled shore
Quoth the Slinger
What were you doing on December 7th?

I wasnt born then.

Nevertheless we must witness this phenomenon
We must have a *Littoral* instance.

I didnt know you had a drawl, Slinger

I dont, I slow up at noon
from the inertia of National Lunch
and from the scatteredness
of the apexed sun which attempts
at that point to enter a paradox —
namely, The West which is The East.

You say the Sun moves!?

Not exactly. Yet when I say what I say,
The Earth Turns.

UmmUm.   That's *Big*, Everything reflected
No *Local* Parallels, admitted the Slinger.
Look ye Everything,
is that a heavy-duty worker
I see at the newstand laughing
into a copy of Scientific American?

It appears so, Master Slinger.

Then we'll question him, Here
he is:
            How, dreamer,
       will fate mark you
in her index when she comes dressed
as a crystalographer
to religne the tumblers
inside your genetic padlock?

Hows that?

He wants to know your name.

Ah yes, how foolish of me,
Dr. Flamboyant, Dr. Jean Flamboyant
I was the flame of my Lyceum
I can fix anything

Anything? said Everything

Anything. Would you like a light
I see yor roach has gone out
continued the Doctor Catching his breath

Slinger, did you flash how
the PHD caught his breath,
never saw anybody do it with their *hand*

Yes agreed the Slinger, Brilliantly fast
Uh thank you puffed the Slinger
youre very polite, Did,
Thanks! Did you take a degree?

May I sit down asked the doctor
fanning his neck
with the Scientific American
and motioning to a bench.

Prie Dieu! the Slinger gestured
with his long fingers, scattering
half the population of the plaza.

Thats right — tho I didnt know it was missed
I **took** a degree
which they had refused to *give* to me

Oh?

Oui. They couldnt find the...
the Object
of my dissertation:
The Tensile Strength of Last Winters Icicles.

You must be joking.

Not at all, it was
that conjectural —
it's whats called a
post-ephemeral subject
always a day late, their error lay of course
in looking for an object

Ah Yes the Slinger mused
When it gets to you
them in their case, me
in mine,
it doesn't exist
Like the star whose ray
announces the disappearance
of its master by the presence of itself.

Correct! That is, within the limits of analogy

Excellent, *Excellent.* Will you join us
Doctor, as we circle the square
of this plaza?

May I accompany you

As you wish, flourished the Slinger

      And so they continued
to walk and to talk
and to discourse on
the parameters of reality.

      And by this process they arrived
at the door of the printers just in time
to greet the Horse quitting
that establishment with a bundle
of parchment.

Hello Horse,
How'd the Auction
go, Kool asked

Not Bad Not Bueno
the Horse laughed
There was some figurante
standin there in a bucket
with crutchs,
he was a "Lucky-Strike Green" fan
so I got the Tall Black
to start a rumor about the statue
was a Hughes disguise
and the fan jumped the bid
from 10 dollars to 20,000

Dollars?!

No. Thats the funny part.
Pounds; this fan was covered
so many ways he got confused.

Fantasía. What happened then?

Well Nothin. It stayed there
Sold to the man in the bucket
with crutchs. I mean
no local was gonna raise that.
So he straps it to the bucket
and takes off.
By the way Slinger
that printers a local printer.

Makes sense, answered the Slinger.

    The Horse then left the set
and began to nail his parchments
around the plaza.

Proclamation

RE: *The CYCLE of*
ROBART'S WALLET

TO THE CITIZENS OF U. C.: THERE IS
IN YOUR CITY TODAY AN ILLUSTRIOUS
TRAVELLER WHOSE EARTHNAME IS
GUNSLINGER AND WHOSE IMAGE YOU
HAVE SEEN AN HOUR AGO DECOACH AT
THE SOUTHWEST CORNER OF THE PIG-
STY YOU CALL YOUR PLAZA. THE GUN-
SLINGER HAVING TURNED THE CONDI-
TION OF THE LOCAL CITIZENRY AROUND
AS HE TURNED HIMSELF AROUND THE
PIGPEN YOU CALL YOUR PLAZA HAS
CONCLUDED THAT THE PRESCRIPTION
FOR YOUR SICK HEADS CAN BEST BE
FILLED BY YOUR PERSONAL ATTEN-
DANCE FIVE MINUTES HENCE IN THE
TANNER'S YARD AT THE S.E. CORNER
OF THIS "PLAZA" TO SEE THE POET RE-
CITE THE ABOVE ALLUSION. YOUR
PRESENCE IS MORE THAN
REQUIRED.

☆

Does that mean we dont have to go
asked one clever voter
of the Horse.

That's *right*, answered the Horse
studying the voter.
If youre as clever as your question indicates
you can stick a dime stamp
on your head
and send it thru the mail — we'll process it
as soon as possible.
But if youre not, I'd advise you
to get your head over there
just like the proclamation says!

THE CYCLE

The Slinger speaks

O Singer, we are assembled here
beneath the rafters of the tanner's shed
Turn the Great Cycle of the Enchanted Wallet
of Robart the Valfather of this race
turn the Cycle of Acquisition
inside the Cobalt Heads of these
otherwise lumpish listeners and make
their azured senses warm *Make* your norm
their own   deliver them
from their *Vicious Isolation*

*W*hereupon the Poet, with one foot forward
released the garmlees

1 I see cars drawn by rainbow-wingèd ſteeds
  Which trample the dim winds: in each there stands
  A wild eyed charioteer urging their flight
  On a long take-off roll, this is the purging of the be

2 Of opulence is the secret Journey, & mad
  Beside him stand Fear and Surrender
  The organic radicals in full salute
  Eager to plunge into the country and keen eyed

3 Covering every exit of the blank hotel
  The perversion of the service elevator
  Of the vacuum of creation and transportation
  Of his unseen symbolic Body *Of* the shrouding

4 In the sacred Commerce of South Station
  Where he walked, exempt of mortal care
  *T*o his leasèd car through the taint of small owners
  And human hands first mimicked and then mocked

5 For *H*e was decoyed as the cheeze in a burger
  Upon a long white stretcher ferried by two poodles
  While he shuffled along with his feet encased
  In kleenex boxes *H*e wobbled astride an industrial br

6 The perfect disguise of the causal janitor
  Who came through Janus from the far side
  From that place where the Mint has its root
  From that place where the Owl has its hoot

7 And human hands first mimicked and then mocked
  Were seen to whisper and were heard pointing
  That gross was the dead certain and random
  And chance lewdness of the multitude

8 Look! The Burger's cheeze, That's it!
  Let's rush the rack and get it back
  Let's turn that cheeze to shit
  Come On! Let's spin a little bit

9 The scene thus leans the way of the stretcher
  As His guard of AntiBasins teleglance
  The Gate and *guard the shuffle* as Save the Cheeze
  Programs through their simple relays

10 And they push all buttons Close all gratings
  Revise all functions Review the digits on The Move
  Repunch the possible Locate the Im
  Feed Back the pragma of the plan Itself

11 This Imperial Fact was tripped
  While Failure drew his plans

12 This one switch was thrown
  While Indignation kicked the throne

13 This cantankerous crowd was led
  To discover how it bled
  By the apparition of a Cheeze, in bed
  And do you know what they said?

14 Do you know what they said? They said
  But He aint never bin seen!
  And he said You maybe oughta look for a bean
  Under at least three shells

15 And that was the Word which nobody heard
   They were into their *Lean* so hard
   So they took two steps back
   And fell into their crack (just like a bucket of lard

16 Well then He smiled and *L*eaned on his broom
   And joined them
   In the dangerous disguise of Nobody
   He ran up a flag of John Adams in drag

17 And a card upon which said *S*tart!
   Here's Being and Time and I'm goosing them good
   And both of ems yours
   For a Dime

18 Did you hear *T*hat they gassed
   We've made it at last
   And they jived and they jived
   And they jived and they jived

19 The green flash struck red
   And one kicker asked as part of the group
   Will you please put it on the loop
   I aint leavin till I get fed

20 So *T*he *M*an throws away his broom
   Like you'd throw away your speech
   So it's Off the Cuff
   Fairly quick, but it's enough

21 To win, and it Does matter how you win
   *S*o for part of the riddle
   He goes into a diddle where He's dressed
   Like a briefcase with its pants down

22 And the rest is invested in a surenough latch
However, His mind was so cool and smart
That he threw away the key and said sweetly
All that I've done I've done only for thee

23 Yet I fear we've been *S*een and *S*urrender
Tells me we must part

24 Goodbye Goodbye as if I
Were a bomb saying Hello to Guatemala or
As if I were a banana saying goodbye to Plato
And as if I were a cherry pit

25 Emerging from the anus of George *Washington*
Goodbye and Goodbye you effect me like a lullabye
Since there's nothing to choose you may do as you please
And as far as I'm concerned you can *K*eep the *C*heeze

26 Then *H*e entered the car which stood along the siding
Its outside as blank as the loin of a Chester White
To hide the pale movements of the Janitor
Who is already strained over the chords of seclusion

27 Who rises now and then pondering the messages
*S*uspending the messengers in the formula
Of another instant
That they may never see, feel and conceive

28 And inhabit themselves for in *N*o *W*ay
May they occupie their instant No matter
How they watch for it
They get sent for Burgers Everytime

29 Also, they are designed to relate
   Rather more with the pickles than with the musta
   For some strange reason

30 But perhaps it is because
   They must be ready at a moments notice
   To *T*ake *Off*, and mustard, whatever it may do
   Has an exceedingly long Take-Off Roll

31 A Fast Head leans over the board
   He's not been seen but you know *H*e's there
   It's Him, the Naked Disposition
   The straight Ray of the Immaculate Attention

32 The direct access to Everyplace
   The means to hold it while He burns its face
   With the hot end of *H*is joint
   And to step around the lurch for the car moves

33 Now the slow exotic periods of the wheels
   Across the sections of track as the car
   Goes over the accordion rails to the Main Line
   The design of the Goddess herself

34 Is tacked to the board as the car tacs
   To the Main Line, this is not about haulage
   Tied up at the dock in ships, this is the Inventory
   And then the Overhaul of the fucking mind!

35 We find 95% of it Unnecessary, He mused
   And Surrender stepped forward right out of his sh
   Is something the matter in there Right Now
   Or is there anything around here you think you can

36 I sure could Pickel: Mustard and catsup
And hold the onion and on your way back
Pick up a Crack
I'm into What Happens when you lose

37 Then when the messenger got off
To the county seat
He turned on the AM and hummed the tune

From the Fall of Anytime

. . . lookout! summers endin Betty
These days are pretty pretty Betty
But theyre a Little colder Betty
Yes theyre a little colder now
And people say if you think
Youre the One
You better not go to Wisconsin Betty
To catch the trees this time around
They say those people aint so glad
They say theyre kinda hoppin mad
Cause they know Why!
They just don't know How they been had

38 What took you so long Surrender
You got the longest roll in the business
Now hand me that Panhandle
And step aside

39 The data the data is spraying the shrine
Start • to ma tremble life was basically a freeload • Stop
That's the simple sense of it refined
From the flak of Biodetail interference

40 That big bleep is the birthday Big Bleep
      Mother's maiden name, the day she choked
      On the apple core No Big Bleep
      This is not gonna go very deep

41 This is a pennsylvania crack, vertical vertical
      Get me another, something up ahead
      And I don't mean Indiana I know where that's at
      Find me a crack from a society with no history

42 Find me a crack that ain't been surrendered in
      Get me a crack from Way up ahead
      All these cracks have already been You Know
      Get me one from Around-the-Bend, somethin goin

43 And the car slipped by the contradictions outside
      The Green and Red and Green and Red
      And as the Globe rotates against the wheels
      The whole thing starts to Rock and Roll

44 And there is nothing more for now to know
      Because the signals speak among themselves
      In an Isolating tongue Red and Green
      And Amber is the medium

45 For it is Amber that his lenses are
      As he sinks in the chair they come out of his head
      Each one revolves to his nose
      So the car moves into the mother train

46 The click of their coupling is as startling
      And as urgent and as quick as a whisper
      Into the ear of a corporate being

With a perfect background, The shrill scream
Of metal to metal across the switch-yard

47 The scream of the Accomplished Present
A conglomerate of Ends, The scream of Parallels
All tied down with spikes These are the spines
Of the cold citizens made to run wheels upon

48 Parallels are just two things
going to the same place that's a bore
He whispers and folds His hands
Nor do His eyes flash inside the Amber

49 They emiT, and the emissions brake
They turn hot red to cold green
They fuck up microreality but good!
No impressions, and like endless kleenex

50 Each datum is caught I got em
And stored cold in a special future
And sent to the floor below
You *Know*, it's a Very short Take-Off roll

51 The prescription of His Amber shades
A mysterium as booby-trapped with counter-locks
Perhaps,
As the multiple entrances to Ft. Knox

52 What has been run thus far
Is what has been run before
Its what can be seen from the floor
It won't make us lock up the store

53 For I once met the decorator of that Interior
   And he pourd a description
   Of that wheelèd apartment
   Into mine ear

54 The trickiest assignment of his life he said
   And one that he'd never declare
   But leave it at this:
   The space has *no* front it's *A*ll rear

The Interior Decorator Runs the Scenario of the Wingèd Car

1 To make all that clear
  Let me unscrew your ear

2 The design problems were insurmountable
  As there was nothing whatever to do
  For you understand that By its nature
  The Rear hangs Wholly behind you

3 The scenario is all Emanation
  The nesting ground of number
  There are no *things* there as such
  Material is a not with the   K   detached

4 All is transhistorical, functions
  Have no date, there is no gear
  The sentient might
  With toothy confidence engage

5 Functions have no date nothing occurs
Dates have no function anyway
Christmas is a tape of Holloween
Every package is a *Bomb*

6 In case you thought all the shit was *Out*
Of Pandora's box at last
There is no light as we get it
Nor any dark as such and the atmos

7 Is the medium of variable tubes of spectra
Like nothing yet gleaned from the Sunne
The condition in there
May not therefore be agnate

8 In other words it could be the One
You know how the species begun
And how the Unique got it off
With his hand

9 Well it's more like that
Which is how it could be
Than it's been since he joined the band

10 Still, there is no-one inside
For inside there is no-One
There is indeed inside only
The No No No

11 And hear the language cleaner
As it sucks up the negatives
From the cracks in the positive linoleum
For this is a large-scale linoleum

12 Inside the Car whose wheels turn
    Opposite to the direction they serve
    Is a man named Al whose codename is Rupert
    Isn't that outrageous

13 Isn't that epistimonical
    Isn't that an appetite for apatite
    What used to be called a deceiving form
    Isn't that the azimuth of the truth

14 This Grand Car with the Superior Interior
    Moves with a basal shift So Large
    It would be a dream to feel time curve
    For no masses so locked serve straight time

15 Thus rhythm has a duty to de-tour the Vast
    Contra Naturum? Baby you ain't heard nothin ye
    Like this is a day in the life
    Of The Man who grabbed the crack

16 And wrapped it around the Antho-space
    From the Eye of the U on out
    Displacement is never felt
    If that's where you're at, uh,
    It looks like that's that

17 I learned that memory here
    Is the mean difference between your shift
    And Star shift
    It's the appetite for apatite
    It's the principle of I feel a storm comin

18 And the sun pops out and all the daisies
    Take off like World Cruisers

Rupert's view of the planet is as
From directly over the N Pole

19 From which point of view Florida
Is about as far south as he can see
Yet equal sense can never clock
The frozen pendulum of such a movement

20 Inasmuch as the Sweep itself
Distinguishes not
Between the Outbound
And the Inbound

21 I didn't receive it as crackproof
Until I located an aperiodic compass
Under that chair He sits in —
Also He's got some primitive touches

22 Like the sundial
Mounted in the palm of His hand
And I don't Know, But They Say
He's got a Star finder in the head of *H*is cock

23 Or used to have

24 It isn't the Eye nor is it the U
The shades are drawn against
The shades are drawn against
The organ of the Imagination

25 Which in Rupert's estimation
Distorts the Interior, turns up the set
When He's only named the game
you know, He AIN'T DELT YET

The I.D. Runs the Actual Furnishings

1 The furnishings are all strictly flat
   That is, if you see a chair to sit in
   You sit in the image of that chair
   You fry an egg in the image of the skillet

2 Which Looks at you like you're Killin it
   Goodbye anything which dares purport To Be
   I myself saw a typewriter filled with concrete
   And raised aloft in instant mockery

3 By *living* Atlantes, a race of half-column half-man
   Who turn each such thing smirking
   dizzying with threats of abandonment
   To gravity
   A basic trick in this uncentered locus

4 Atlantes also hold the drawn shades down
   And they open and close the rear door
   When Fear and Surrender come and go
   On their unscheduled excursions

5 And these Atlantes pick the pockets
   Of the passing guard producing almanacs
   Or tintypes of Brigham Young in drag
   But they cannot count

6 Neither do pictures constitute an image
   In their plaster heads, In any case
   They mostly make a gesture of disgust and wink
   Which is always a chain reaction among them

7 When they speak they say simply Shit!
Or thanks! though sometimes they whine
Could I have the pickle when youre done with it?

8 Their conversational English is limited
Yet they mimick its rehearsal very cleverly
They fear one thing and one thing only
And that is the avaricious Vice-Versas

9 An obscene and gluttonous order of rat
The Supreme Janitor unleases on the floor
After Lunch where they destroy themselves
With madness

10 When they find nothing
But their Raving Expectations
And upon this Nought
They bloat and bloat and bloat

11 And Rupert cackles and grabs for Breath
And hollers This!
Is what we keep the slums awake with

12 And then, there is the Atlante who holds
A special position the one
With the fixed Astral Grin
Detested by all the others

13 But not because he is Rupert's favorite
In his hand he holds a tablet as a waiter
holds a tray
And upon the tablet rests an urn

14 Which in turn bears the inscription
        EMIT NO TIME
   Cut in a lascivious style around its liprim
   Yet around the base is cut
   An even greater impudence
        MADE IN JAPAN

15 Inside this urn are the ashes
   The final remains of a colossal clock
   Which stood in the hallway
   At the beginning of Organized History

16 And the sound started out as a Tock
   But quite soon it settled down as a Tick
   It possessed no face so it couldnt be traced

17 And this Atlante whos name is Al
   After his master did a number which went
        Four Five Slow
        Four Five Slow
        Three Four Low
        Three Four Low
        Three Four Five
        Three Four Five   Through chorus after cho

18 His eyes are sunk from the perpetual
   Debauchment of gross scorn
   He pours into the urn with his eye
   Onto the ashes of the Idea of Time

19 Under his left ear he bears
   The cuneiform form of Man
   And below his right ear the mark of God
   And these were the signs of his predicament

20 For his head was caught like a pod
    Between this nasty pair

21 And he wasted Rupert by seeming
    To tip the Urn *too far*
    And he likewise drove the other Atlantes wild
    Whose coats had been pulled

22 That if Time is spilled in a gravityless space
    And becomes equally distributed
    That is if an absolute symmetry occurs
    And inertia is total
    That's as heavy as shit in suspension can get

23 So it sure kept their form sacerdotal
    With unending regret that the inscription
    Was not quite the same backwards as forwards
    And Although they detested him

24 Because he treated the whole Interior
    As if it were a cloakroom
    They were always excited
    By the way he provided a rundown

25 Take One, he'd begin,
    That was what in Olden Times
    Was called a perfect mistake, *The Singularity*
25ª You know how Supermorph here
    Got into Meta-physics?

26 Well he's got *such* a short take-off roll
    That he was usually Up before
    The front end got off the ground
    So if anything went wrong He was

27 *Still up* when the nose went down
    Oh Children! *The hour has struck by the clock*
    Don't mean shit to him

28 He's got this rag clock
    With a yellow shag
    He keeps um under his pillow
    He talks to um to keep um awake

29 Pay *A*ttention he screams then bites um
    And spits minute words in ums ears
    Very small words in ums ears
    This is no *hypothetical radical* sweetheart
    This is a *systematic arrangement* like salt

30 This junk is out the back door
    And as youve Heard there's only the rear here
    Meta Meta   Meta Meta
    Mount the thing before that mother

31 Or one of his clones hits the button,
    Lest he mete and dole
    You all better roll and wrap
    Your finger around the Cola Coka

32 Glug your dugs but don't drap it
    It'll break your Base and you'll, Um
    Come in riffin your kneecaps like
    You're involved in some world-wide shit

33 Wink! But Cocaine, oh sure
    There's a national experience
    Would you Bolivia that? It's inside your heads
    Alright like a blackboard eraser

34 Its always On The Other Hand
   Or futher datadata could uh Verify
   If you lift the lid you'll get to the toilet
   Oh my neglected field of stunted glories

35 You sure got transferred to the side crack
   Oh my frozen beauties that rap's
   Not funny, Forgive me to the futurePast
   And he fell silent and shed a tear

36 Like a ball of jasper it rolled
   Into the mouth of a Vice-Versa and disappeared
   And the Atlantes listend to the disturbing silence
   In the eyes, the haunted eyes of Rupert's favorite

37 And Rupert sat still behind his slick lids
   And the subtlest twitch he made
   Because he was as proud, brother, as a dog
   With two tails

38 While in the fits of his astral vision
   Al the Atlante paced the Hall with his dumb eyes
   Dear friends you've gotta know I'm sad
   Where where Where have they got us
   Where is the crack where they've put us

39 We have got no feet!
   That's the cruel fucking fact Atlantes
   Look at yourself HEADLINES
   Power Struggle in Drop City

40 So when he hits the button
   You all better make sure your pedestal
   Ain't made out of nothin organic um
   Looks like you Wooden types will have to go

41 *Oh, Al,* we've got a *tacktical problem* here *Al*
We've got a tacktical problem here Al
The Atlante numbered 19 changed the subject
Yes Al, something for the crimestoppers

42 Came over the wire you know
Something going on here
Of an epicene gender Al
In a Epicœne fury
Very Very ἐπικοινος
« Get it over with 19! »

43 Oh Hum Yess Yess
It's whether or not
You can scan the plot
«You know you can do as you choose 19!»

44 Yes, I figure that's on
Since this Dawg in the door
Is flashing his scar and pointing down thar
But it's whether or not you can scan the plot

45 And make it fast Which came by last?
I mean Big Richard was holding the Pot
I mean, Now, we know he's *Held* it

46 Shut up 19! Rupert snapped on
And moved his amber shades
Like a sweep from the conning tower
And His finger poised over the button

47 Which could activate the Vice-Versas
And either way it's far out   how

He cons the present to hustle the futchah
By a simple elimination of the datadata

48 Which was unpunched and resealed
And into the system came the muse
Singing   Used War for Sale
As down from the rear came the message

49 I think this is it Boss
The crack we been waitin for
The scanners have picked off
A telegram to Parmenides

50 From a point on the arc
2 days minus 4 Corners
We sure know where that's at Boss, um
We can find it *in the Dark*

O Poet! the sun like a sword
Cuts below the *Tanner's Yard*
and we must hear the effect formed
of the code name Rupert another time
Another time we will witness
how this double hydrocarbon hustles the future
but for now,
Fresh *Distortions* have swept the screen
And from the smell brought in by the winde
we have news of the Master Nark
who trailed us into your cycle
Yet there is another, an *Unknown*
who tracks us
Someone whose *fame* is his *Name*

A summer storm advances Though it is autumn
You will conclude in another Town
away from the Shades
*W*hen under the cool *S*trokes of *Muthos*
we'll find out about
which way that Epaćtos goes

BOOK
III

*The inside real
and the outsidereal*

for Harvey Brown

The Lawg

Contained in the brain
like the nose was invented by cocaine
is the sum of What
Slam that filing cabinet shut!

Here Kums the Kosmos
Dont just stand there! (lookin dumb
Stick out your thumb.

The Body in winter is the hunting lodge
deep in the forest sheltered, with a view
overlooking the full metaphor of the hart
and before all else in the winter interior
before winde and snowe
and before you goe
or when you suddenly are the guest of time
where the afterbirth of space hangs
in the mirror of rime
and where one place
is the center of this terrific actualism
  the waves of simplicity cross
    the shoals of destiny
      the shadows a
        cross the top of your grand desk
          are the numbers of your Winter Book
            the tumblers of the opening falling
          opening the Gates of Capricorn, the
        days have decreased as much as they ever will
      snowe covers living things with quietude
    Death rules over the visible, then,
Life surges with the Sunne out of decline
  the Sunne moves northward the light tauter
    spring spreads the New Life over cool death
      and the dissected earth includes the contrary
        over which our heads are not pervasive
          for there the nightforce increaseth
          "a rite
          not of passage
          but penetration

          a cellular destruction

          an act
          of will"

the maneuvers of a brilliant ghost
who returns with a longer stride
in his eye
        Apparently,
we wobble
several important periods show it
There is no vacuum in sense
connection is not by contaƈt
sense is the only pure time
connection is a mechanical idea
nothing touches, connection meant is
Instant in extent a proposal of limit

   Dear lengthening Day
I have loved your apparencies since you created me

The Winterbook

For some while we parallel the train
whose shining rails are closed at both horizons
and this group in which our brain
is contained, speakes in the excellent tones
of the beginning of an ascent, feel them rising
into the realm of the surprising
bent over what they say
along the river Rio Grande
'earing the low chordes of the foothills
spitting the seeds of the Sandias
out of the corners of their eyes
as they rise
towards the land of the crazy Utes
over and thru the mordants
of the bridges and the buttes

Has Anybody got any Simple Class
the Slinger enquired of the complicated group
or is this road not
"on the road." Someone
bumped by the Rational
could get on a plea
for unencumbered forward motion
because since I got here
I've been issued every ball of twine
your poor molecules can combine
from A to C

Whad you get for B Everything asked politely

Bullshit the Slinger replied
and the sign to Santa Fe grazed his vision
This Tampiqueño imprisons my head
in a pre-Cornel Wilde timeblock
I'm too inside oilrigs
and big assed gents from Corpus Christi

Well now that I know the location, Señor
I'll alight in Santa Fe later in the day
to score a lid, what say you

I picked it up the Slinger said
as L.W. Lyde, Manchester 1935,
who said, Pindar did
A large portion of his work
under the influence of the Emotional
light — in the early hours
and in the late hours of the day

Youll need tiptop growth
Everything began to say
because your head
is almost out of-the-way
like as in some farflung passion play

I see us
going thru the village of Placitas
the poet interrupted, Slinger?
Do you forsee the Master Nark
interpreting our route

Thats not possible to say
returned the Slinger swaying in the coach
He's so complicated he believes
the shortest distance between two states
is a straight line
and since he's travelling on roller skates
I'd say he'll be there ahead of time
or shortly thereafter and since a icecream cone
is what he'll be inside
it's not exactly likely
that we'll collide, here
take a look, the Slinger says
holding up a handmirror

No thanks the poet refused
the place I could have used that
was in the village
we just left behind, a kind of Mexican hat
you know where thats at!

Dont push your luck
the horse advised
Theres less to that village
than meets your eyes

Thanks a lot Lévi-Strauss
Thats typically wise
and by the way Slinger
since our horse is so NIZE
will you speak a response
to the request "build me
a better genetic louse-trap"
and then we can take
our morning nap

BUILD ME A GENETIC LOUSE TRAP
yawned the Slinger
— Better, the poet corrected
Let's see, that sounds Mercenary
But, THE HORSE is a wringer for memory
and because we're here
you can understand this hemisphere
was initiated to Europa's myths
by this creature whome we've learned to steer

Get Away ! the Horse had to say

He pranced across the Incas
and now he puts down the fincas
He is wherever power is flexed I notice
except in the sea for he's too small there

He's the one who
NEVER LOOKED AT THE CAMERA, thats ex camera
He is the companion of aftermath
thats post-numeral
He's the one who studied war itself
before the invention of the path
Your horses personify the striving after knowledge
the road along which we drive symbolizes

       (you are aware Symbolize
              and Personify
        is a mimicry of Earth Habits,
          The Slinger said aside

Symbolizes our thinking process

Sagittarius is the art of memory the Arrow
The brother is the horse of mem
                       -ory
The horse is the brother of woman
The brother of Mother Memory
you know, the lady who runs the hot-dog stand

       Thats an elegant geneology
the Poet whispered into the ear
of the risen morning Sunne
as the stormclouds covered it
and the Horse smiled perceptibly
and asked the Slinger Do you REMEMBER ME?
dont you have something else to say?

OH Jack, the Slinger prayed
I want you to feel
and in your feeling move your bones
for the want we now have of your access
in this time so little beyond you
and which needs your moving nerve
as it dries tacked
on the warp of its own flat sedimentary internalism
>   The divisions of hunger
>   shut behind their Doors
>   Pinned down by their Stars
>   Kept going by their Rotors
>   Waked up by their Alarms
>   Attended by a Prose
>   which says how Dead they are
>   Frozen by a Brine
>   which keeps them from Stinking
>   It looks to me Jack
>   like The Whole Set is Sinking
>   And theyre still talkin œcology
>   Without even Blinking

Ah Men, saith the Horse

Here comes Indica Jack
He's got his gnosis in a sack on his back

Now, repeat after me 20 times

>   I promise my mother
>   I will not join the Sierra Club

Wild Horses! Everything promulgated
What kinda mother you got

Are you serious? She's a horse
Naturally

Of course, of course —
AND, you dont want none
of your sacred quatrapeds
packin no Honky Bi-peds
to the top of no sierras
for a look at whats
left of their more prominent hysterias!

Everything, you have got an Instant sense
is what the Horse could feel
in récompense

And Everything like a Simple Worker
had his wares laid out
Announcing that the flipside always comes
as the light snowe
casually attracted to the earth
drifting blew
thru the perfumery of the piñon clad hills
which flash on the frames
of the windows of our journey
and cause the junipers to go by

Poet, me senses
say you have in you
something Low this morning

fewer stairsteps
support your duel
You stare out the window
at the peasants gathering fuel on the hill
have ye banked yor fires
wheres the Fairbanks
of your desires?
In your eyes I see
the underground
like a miner with his lamp
turned around

        The weather in the winter the poet nodded
is a circulated mound
the great policer of the glaciers
intermission from the cruel isotherms
He hunts the land, and
all things there on
And because the soul of man
must always seek a warm tit
he tends to like his summer fine
"Light and Darkness, thats it"
we 'ear from Parmenides, in frag. 9

And he TENDS to get in line
as long as the sign above the booth reads

SUBLIME
STARRING THE MAN
(sold out)

Yor imagery is sensational
the Slinger interrupted the singer
But you know, it's also associational —

Listen, my celestial friend,
We've got it from the Man
on the 9th floor
who has been lookin all over the Milky Way
for a Mars Bar like you
if only to confirm his faith
in the Monte Carlo Procedure

And he has declared his crosshair
at 2 days minus 4 corners

$37°$ North
$109°$ West
more or less

That's Associational

PROJECTIONS OF THE FUTURE BORE ME
like back in Olde Towne & beyond
the Slinger spat
you know why everybody
in this state's fat?
They're convinced torque
is a relationship
between the tongue and the fork
now you know where thats at!

I do said the poet
and I sure heard the third rime
they want it all the tine

Continue then
with the construction of your sets
each piece fits

      So, like the mind goes foward to
the Hoodoos, sabe?
to the site of their theoretical looming
           It is the load above
           it is the hod-carrier
           of the head, love

What was It doing there?
It sat on the trap door
        in the floor
then It laid down this very strange backtrack
and It got
to thinking so wide
Eats head
went out the side of the room
        of the room
and moved the stadium
to declare its connections
and the flashy scoreboard read
THE OUT*OF*TOWN TEAM IS VERY MODAL
   THEREFORE THIS SHIT COULD BE

TOTAL

VAroom ! he said
Whats that?
The room he said
whats that
a bloom he said
oh whats that
the Bloom he said
Oh what is that
Kartoum he said
oh what is THAT
it is the Imperial bloom he said
what is it?
Outside the room they said
What, Whats outside?
Everything says it must have come
from under his hat!
I agree with Everything the Horse said
we'll have to look into that!
The Imperial bloom is waht prompted him
to go into the room and put on Bruckner
as the sun was going down
like into the basement of walt disneys asshole
What, whats outside?
The outside, the OUTside the chorus chorused

So then, Slinger it is still not known
how deeply you have studied
this lingual springer
of the western Kind
how we came past the methadrain
and how the war was begain

and now falls out on them hoodos in the rain
in those hodos under the sunne . . .

As the sapien who peels
his lupus vulgaris
in the light of the moon
is inferior to the scandian loon
So he is superior
to the mammal in the reading room
who can't build a scaffold
without losing his head
and who Does Not feel
his philosophy when it drops
    but who has an abstract in his case
of a portable myſtery
before which he is harangued
to stay awake!
lest he move his whadayacallit
into the line of his spine

a curve of some grace
it could serve as a place
from which to go thru

I mean the excellence of the yew bow

      Just so, the auditory Slinger returned
There are some reasons why
I am taken by the beauty of your number
yet repelled by your device
and the energy of your pseudodox

To a poet all authority
except his own
is an expression of Evil
and it is all external authority
that he expiates
this is the culmination of his traits
Thus my mission on position seven
is Inspector of the Grates
Like when the fire goes out here I'll report back
AND AHEAD
It is my fate you might say
to occupy position eleven
the same way I do seven

But whats this?
the Horses of Instruction
have made the grade outside Mádrid
tho they crave no more effort
than a hickory winde

                    Me sees
past the curtain
a certain destruction
the hills have been upended
theyre no longer blended upon
the plates of their own dynamic principles
could a lover have done this, hombre?

          I dare not say
but while the coach was dark
and I had, combined, the circumference
of Our Mind, a stark alignment of the Sunne
Ourselves and the Moon occurred

And
when the lunation was screened
I had this vision which came in
as a poem called

The Poem Called
Riding Throughe Mádrid

I shall speak it —

When next you visit The World

Talk with the Trees and
Speak into the Trees and
Get it on with the Trees
They know whats happening
Over the hill of time

Stand up in the Trees
They go straight to heaven
And they have heaved in waves
Their deposits in earth

The miner has brought up
The madder from their graves

They have made the vanes and
They have made the stage
And it is only they
Who have given their flesh
    To this thing
        And this ring
            And this ring

The Horse then made a Gong!
with his shoes
                    And Lil
began to choose from her case
a star from the flowering tree space
and out of the storm
there came a chickadee
who sat on her wrist
for a while
and brought a smile to the Horse
whose feet were still tingling
from the gonging

You have made my ears remember
        "the world soul
            slumbers in matter"
the Slinger quoted
                    and added

Slap in a tape
of my second favorite group
we'd best relieve this little troupe
if that machine is worth its quartz
with TH' EUROPEAN SON TO DELMORE SCHWARTZ

        And the coach runs smartly now
by the torn rooves of this company town
while the tabla of the 4 & 20 hooves
and the run run run of the sound
brings the cognition
of our psychomorphs around
So now, the Slinger says
We're Cerrillos bound

Just then a goggled bi-plane pilot
hung from a pure hemp line
across the window like a pendulum do
waving a night letta
with the sheepskin glove of his hand

Then let him in the Slinger suggested
and the pilot swung through the door
Havent we seen you before?
Lil conjured

You might have, I used to be
the chisel holder to Praxiteles
Now I'm the messenger to the secretary to Parmenides

Was that a promotion? Lil asked aside

And I have brought you the data
in this here night letta

uhHuh, whats back of it?

The One

uhHuh, whats that?

A tricky plea
to deny
the 'other' hand of reality

Is that the code?
No that's the imagery
          The Code
is Sllab —

I'll take a stab the Slinger said
Who's that

There is but one Sllab ahead
(don't look back
and Bean is his messenger

We have reckoned that
the Slinger said
From the shape of your head
What else?

Sllab has a Double Trough Æntenna
from which he gets his information
the Pilot reported
Here's a random sample

      — Kick out the Dickel
         a hard bunch of consumers
         is comin through the door

Does Sllab know
the æntenna is fucked

Maybe it aint, Anyway
That's not the biggest key
all his data
is based on WHAT THEY SAY

Moreover he leases the data
to an activity called HooRay
which went right on down
to produce a group

with such a heavy assay
it was called Western Man
or, Imprudential Behavior
it was a real flash in the pan
but, you know, that had this hit like

       Waffle Time!
and you must recall their early side

LET'S SPEND AN AFTERNOON ON THE MOON
  DIGGIN IT UP WITH A SPOON AND SOON
   THE EARTH WILL RISE
  TO OUR GREAT SURPRISE
WHILE YOUR HAND ON MY HOOD
  IS GONNA FEEL REAL GOOD   ¿

What a title!
How does the lyric goe?

How would I know!
I gotta go now, Buena suerte!
and the pilot swung out
on his Pure Hemp Line
and was winched up to his bi-plane

        O, are you gonna open
        the Night Letta Slinga
the chorus asked

Once we're away from Santa Fe
we'll see what the
Secretary to Parmenides has to say

But now
            A weak-minded mammal stands
on the corner of his head
and fort Phil Korny avenue
you can catch him
as the Driverless Horses pull in
this must be Everything's connection
whos haranguing the perspicacious crowd
'But why is he so loud' Lil asked
'perhaps he can use some help
before he gets boxed up and sent North

      May I ask you a question
the subject asked
with his head in the window
and his finger sticking in his muthos
or have you got the time?

A fast nickel beats a slow dime, Jim

      Well, uh, the world is absolutely finite
and the cosmos is indefinitely finite
whats that?

a cross between a billiard table
ana sponge cake the Horse whispered
in Lil's piercèd ear

YOU HAD HELP!
Here! catch, and Everything woke up with a big Hell
just in time to grab the gramme

Hello Everything, the Horse said
as his left eye lockt on Slinger
What makes Process and Reality heavy
      is the &!

Slinger shouldn't we
oughta hear that Night Letta
before we Blow Up?

Makes sense the Slinger agreed
as he opened the letta
and commenced to read

REPORT GX &C
the Public Version
THE SECRETARY TO PARMENIDES SENDS
THE NIGHTLETTA VIA THE BIPLANE

The phone on the stagecoach wall then Rang
and the Horse picked it up
February 31ſt ! he said into the mouthpiece
Lévi-Strauss here
Ah, Flamboyant
Youre in Beenville, is that a place
or THE FLATULENT TENSE

     And at this precise moment
Dr. Flamboyant began to arrive
in a Turing Machine
one automatum at a time

What's this a toe and an ear?
the Slinger asked and put on the speaker
with a snap of his finga

     Anyway Flamboyant your voice sparkles
   like a zircon
Nice of you to say that Lev
I've been working on the 3 Great Beenville Paradoxes

State them the Slinger requested
the tape's awinding
like J. Edgar Whoever is on Crank

    Thanks for the extra attention
Flamboyant crackled and began

Take 1 of 3 of the Great Beenville Paradoxes
        Nature abhors a vacuum
        but for nature, A VACUUM'S
        GOT NOTHING AT ALL

Take 2 of 3
        To be in Beenville Was
                IS
        To be in Beanville still

Take 3 of 3
        The vacuum ADORES Nature
        for heers abhoring

Thats straightforward enough
the Slinger commented, Waht's
Heers?

Thats a combining form used
here to circumscribe It, but wait

        there is a matching set of pseudoparadoxes

pseudo P(a
        Time and Life cooperate once a week, or used to

pseudo P (b
    Muy Señores Nuestros
    the mass of me you have in your coach
    can never be longer
    than yesterday's roach

pseudo P (c
    Everything is prehensible
    for from that which is not
    we fall off

Thanks a lot Flam Everything murmured

Dr. Flamboyant, the Slinger asked
what is the condition of Pseudo P (b

a "Garden of Eden Pattern"

uh Huh, your hand has arrived
shall we shake it?

        Whew! I don't know, this Turing Machine
I'm travelling in has a worn timing chain
I need a digital transient recorder Bad
the main mass of me which waits here in Beenville
decided to phone ahead, quite without
the authority of the Whole Body
so my head might still be here when you arrive
Just bring what you receive of my body
in a safeway paper bag marked BEANS
I'm trying to convince someone here
I'm a Traditionalist

Four-ten! Doc, will do
but dont hang it up yet
the Slinger has some questions about the set

Et bien, put him in

Slinger here, Doctor Flamboyant
What's the Garden of Eden's function
in Beenville

None whatever, this is a contingency observation
from WHATS LEFT OF ME in Beanville

   Youre getting configurations
that cannot arise in a game
because no preceding generation can form them
They appear only if given in the zero generation
Because such a configuration has no predecessor
it can not be self reproducing — in otherwords
Pat it on the back, give it something to eat
put it in a crib, and tell it it looks sweet

   I follow you the Slinger puzzled
but arent you the predecessor?

ONLY IN BEENVILLE, Flamboyant shouted

Ah yes, the Slinger smiled
the Pre-emption of the Ultra-specific!
but how do I know which one of you to consult?

See pseudo P lowercase c

Thank you! uh, don't you loose something
when you transmit your self serially?

Everytime, but not Everything,
        Once I lost my keys
                and couldnt get in
        Once I lost my knees
                and couldnt get down
        Once I lost my face
                and couldnt frown
        But I've never lost my place
                and that's why work it
                I'm still around

Muy Muy insoportable
the whole group chorused

By the way Slinger Flamboyant asked
Did you get the Night Letta
of which I got a carbon
brought here by the goggled biplane pilot?

Yas!

Will you need help with it?

Perhaps, how do you think it feels?

DoeKnow, I wired for clarification
and I sent the following help
        I know all I have written
        I have not written all I knows

Seventy six!

Affirmative the Slinger nodded
taking up the night letta
as the phone went dead
Now he said lets hear what I said:

THE SECRETARY TO PARMENIDES
SENDS THE NIGHTLETTER VIA THE BIPLANE

REPORT BGX + QUAD III [2 D'S - 4 C'S]
EARTH FOR TRANSMISSION DEEP SECTION
REF. "EMISSION POSITION 9" CLEAR PAST
HOURS PRESENT TIME ALIEN PLANTATIONS
REVERSE SENSE EE GEE ROWS B TO Z DECADE
7 NATION 23 TERMINAL DISPOSABILITY
SKIP SIMPLE NULLIFICATION NO HIT STOP
HIT PROCESS: STRICTLY FRONTBRAIN DEX-
TROROTARY EQUATIONS: SPECULATION
SIMULATOR NAILS FOLLOWING PROBATE ON
PROGRESSIVE WHOOPEE CURVE: ACTUAL
NUMBERS — IRREVERSABLE PREFIX LINE
LITERAL NUMBERS — FLATRAP INFORMATION
TEETOTTER

WORKING RESULT: IDENTICAL BUILT-IN
"NOOSE" EFFECTS PREDICTED AS IN OC-
CASIONS 12&3 OF JUMBLED PAST [REPT.
GX + -2, WORKS]

WE [1ST SYNTHETIC ENTITY SERIES] AN-
TICIPATE [LOCAL MISTAKE] ABSOLUTE
LINGUATILT SURVEY SITE #1 TIMEROOF
[JERKWATER IMAGE] STEP – THIS – WAY
EFFECT RELATIVE DISLOCATION: PARAL-
LEL SURVEY ASSURES COLLOQUIAL LOCKS
HOLD AGAINST ANY METHOD APPLIED OUT-
SIDE TIME: THE LINE FOR LITERAL NUM-
BERS STABLE WITHIN WIDE PRESENT FRAME
– ALL PRESENT SCHEMA KNOWN CONFORM
LOCAL STRANDS: SET BIOLINES AT GROSS
BODY MOTIONS: RADICAL CONFORMATION
CURVED TO SURVIVE SPLITTING .78 IN-
TERIOR VECTORS AT "WATCH IT!" FRE-
QUENCY # 4: COMPENSATE STIMULATED
DRIFT CONTINENTAL SLAVES BY FACTOR 10
SQUARES [STANDARD SIGNAL + 4]: LIN-
GUATILT PROVIDES TONAL EQUIVALENT FOR
HABIT: REAL NUMBERS UNSTABLE IN CLASS
1 & 2: EXPECT MATERIALIZATION AT PRE-
CISELY 4 CORNERS

REGARDS TO EVERYTHING

SECRETARY TO PARMENIDES

BOOK
IIII

for Jeremy Prynne

Prolegomenon

 oddesse, excellently bright,
thou that mak'st a day of night.
You tell us men are numberless
and that Great and Mother
were once synonymous.

« We are bleached in Sound
    as it burns by what we desire »
and we give our inwardness
in some degree to all things
but to fire we give everything.

We are drawn beneath your fieryness
which comes down to us
on the wing of Eleusian image,

and although it is truely a small heat
our cold instruments do affirm it.
So saith Denis, the polymath.

We survey the Colorado plateau.
There are no degrees of reality
in this handsome and singular mass,
or in the extravagant geometry
of its cliffs and pinnacles.

This is all water carved
the body thrust into the hydrasphere
and where the green mesas give way
to the vulcan floor, not far
from Farmington and other interferences
with the perfect night
and the glittering trail
of the silent Vía Láctea
there is a civil scar
so cosmetic, one can't see it.

A supcrimposition, drawn up
like the ultimate property
of the ego, an invisible claim
to a scratchy indultum
from which smoke pours forth.

But now, over the endless sagey brush
the moon makes her silvery bid
and in the cool dry air of the niht
the winde wankels across the cattle grid.

Book IIII

Then went through the Superior Air
a descension in summer from the troposphere
over the high mountains
and along the Colorado Plateau
dry and warm, the fairest
and rarest mood
of the southwest earth

And the currents of fragrant oil
disperse in the hills like greek wine
    Only at the rim
    does the day tremble & shine.

With the self-protecting instinct
of a surgeon at an inquiry
Robart let the document fall open
Ordnance, Municiones, he muttered

The Global report fell continuous
from the wire into his hand
It was the braille version
which he read with his finger tips
as with his other hand he read the menu
and laughed long and loud
He was riding backward . . .
I has returned from the cultural collective
his fingers told him

An artificial bird twittered
on the theoretical window sill

A digital smile swept his lips
Robart took up a Sullivan
and Al stepped forward
working the wheel of a feudor
not quite out of his shoes
in fact, Al has got rather slow
since coming to Colorado

Robart ordered a Steffansson Special
one quickly grilled lamb
but he departed from the classic menu
by having some bread, a roll,

This roll's as hard as a rock, he sang

it amused Robart to eat bread
that was his way of identifying
with the masses
Keeping in touch he called it

He chewed his meat very thoroughly
and swallowed it
with a Very Great Deal of Thot
trying the various chain messages
of the animal's day,
caterpillars big as tractors
the strange garlic of the herders
the dewy mornings in the sweet Utah hay
the buzz of the massive afternoons

then abruptly picked up the courvoissier
and spit it into a waiting basin
#19 held before him
for Robart used liquor Strictly for mouthwash.
And then with an electric mutter
he began to plan
a major invasion of the modality

Plaise the Lord
and pass the municiones Al chortled
Have you read that nasty note from the Xah?

Shadup you impudent slave Robart grinned
and balanced a kleenex on the tip of his nose

You the onliest man in the world
can do that boss, Al sang

You say that because it so true, Albert

No patrón I say that
because you got the only special
rigid kleenex in the unit

That's what I like about you Al
youre smart, youre independent
youve got class
youre the Robert Taylor
to my Lee J Cobb

Uh, Honey, Al whispered
I know it's a big move to change the subject
SUBject Robart Spewed
That's another thing I like about you Al
youre So traditional

Uhhuh, nevertheless Ducks,
whats on the chain
now that it's obvious to the Opposition
how much we been blue-shifted

Don't worry your plaster head
Al, we can turn this car
into a chile relleño
in a mere fraction of Nothin Flat!
Yesah, but it's always 60 feet long
an on wheels

You misjudge this population Albert
theyll think it's experimental

Eeow!, like the Toronto La Crosse Club?

Exactly, more not less
and what with the Shortage Industry
wirkin thre shifts
theyll just think it's Something to Eat

and as for wheels
Ive wired Akron for a full set of tortillas,
Total Agony!

Slicks? Superslicks, no surface At All
and anyway, parkins easy in Scratchback
In sum, I don't see any trouble
at the Big End so long
as we keep the error-box empty, Now
take care of this communique
and what say
we double the order on the fireworks
of nostalgia

Gums & resins, brimstone
naphtha and the other bitumens
and uh more salt petre & sulphur
benzol & potassium, dont forget
the ducks grease
and pass me that dish of Radio poo
you got there by your elbow
and oh yes, one gross
CO_2 pellets
a battery of HeNe lazers
one mobile Rulz Field Beam
What's that last item, Boss?
#19 inveigled

That's the sow, we'll
use it to hold the property lines
when the maribunta pour in

Al stepped forward
right off his plinth

and add a ton of Traen Oil
and a pot big enough to boil it up
just in case we need to give
those Mogollones a bath
and find out if they got any
OT in this trivium
We're gonna have Order
Even if we have to inject it.
Those types are itching
for the court of piepowder
and altho they were once amusing
this is no time
for technological sentiment
weve got to put those dusty feet
on the path to oblivion —
did you know we've cornered the short-time fuses?

But Pet, a lot of those Single Spacers
is what you fondly called
your Glorious Low-Violence Army
Now you want to soakem
in all this draino?

We're Scientists Al, Sometimes
we have to do Things we hate
Things that even sicken us
You remember, when we was red-shifted
how sick I got
when I had that sharp focus view
of the Great Beyond
we were in motion ahead of the velocities
like the tachyon

Well, now it's all backfire
and we're sucked again through the Dust Veil
and I see the Pleiad
just gathering for breakfast
at the Café Sahagún,
pass me that pick-up cone
and me goggles
and man the toggles

      In the Café Sahagún
in downtown Cortez, Colorado
our party assembles
from out of the thin air

I comes thru the door
twirling his psychognosis
in his fingers
and throws it at affective intervals
into the air
like a texas cheerleader
and when he drops it behind his back
which is quite often, according to the formula,
he turns around to pick it up
with a dainty bending of the knees
and an expression of Oh-that-doesnt-matter
on his vibrant lips
as he hums Just for today
I will not be afraid
and I will enjoy murdering
now that I can perform
all by myself, an act of oblivion

What do you want for Breakfast
the manager shouted

Give me a drum roll
and a symbol crash!
I glared thru the propeller of his baton

He shoulda stayed in Greece
Everything muttered
he's coked out to his ears
and he's spewing with chewing gum

      Hello Everything, thought you'd
Never get here
HI there Lil, did you all
keep me in minde, oh Looke
I wish I had some of Those Things
Everything's eating

That's a dish of Etzalqualiztli!
Lil said, extending her hand
Corn & beans

Fascinating, I said, taking it

Everything you got Produce
all *Over* your lapel, say
whats that other bowl of matter
stationed before you
like a Hollywood award

Crawfish pie, Everything shuddered

Crawfish pie is frozen for Certain
in Cortez, Everything, I nodded
so *that* should get you right for Apache time.

Oh is this Apache time, Everything doubted

No it's sublime time I screamed
Los cajeros llena menguante nueva
Deevine. Ay yi yi yi, ay yi yi yi
I sang and motioned for the check

That's where I fell in love
when stars above came out to play
Did you all know the athapascans
had no word for red?
Now that's confidence!

Entrapment is this society's
Sole activity, I whispered
and Only laughter,
can blow it to rags
But there is no negative pure enough
to entrap our Expectations

So what you all been up to
in this land of endowed monks

Rockin Along, Everything gesticulated
Dr. Flamboyant blew his struts
but he xld be along soon

Yes I heard that I said,
glazed with amazement when the manager
kicked the table with a smirk
and presented the check
which turned out to be a series
of characters written on his index finger
which he stuck in Everythings Ear

Everythings eyes spun.
Two plumbs, the manager shouted
hanging on to Everythings tongue
too bad you only got two eyes
youd make a fair bandit

A 50 Caliber Derringer
sprung out of I's right sleeve
and drilled two test holes
in the managers skull

Whaaâ, Everything stammered
as the manager hung by a finger
from Everythings ear

It's OK I said, theres *no* Ban
on mobile weapons, *remember?*
Salt talks,
or as Dr. Johnson said:
if Public war be allowed
to be consistent with morality
Private war must be equally so

I don't give a fuck about that
Everything panicked, get this
finger outa my ear

Um, zymosis of the brain, I observed
peering thru the managers head
But whats this I said
Those two flies mating on the opposite wall
were clean on line, still sittin there
strapped together
there must have been some Irregularity
in the managers head
I shoulda used a Pepperbox
But let's talk Process, not Content

Robart will be trying to cut
our ion source, Said the Slinger
looking thru the window, *whats that*
stickin outa your ear, a finger?
Yea, it belongs to that manager
down there on the floor,
I had to cut it off his hand

Where's our poet the Slinger asked

Oh yes, Lil said, *he's up ahead*
Went to meet Taco Desoxin,
they just brought
Tonto Pronto, down from Toronto
to meet Dr. Flamboyant, if he's able
to reassemble hisself there,

Theyre going to cross the cross
Theyre working out their theory
of the chic ground loop,
the original art of which
is rumored to be "eminently rapid"

and depends on the difference between
Saying and singing, Tonto Pronto
is the World Famous ear specialist

Well have him take a look at Everything
I can't live with that finger in his ear
it's just too conspicuous
But what else can Tonto Pronto do, Lil?

What can Tonto Pronto do?
Oh No, Tonto Pronto dont do *anything*
but so far he's told us Robart just passed
into the Scratchback purview
and when we asked him how he knew it
he said he Heard *im do it*

The lonely wail of the old Cannonball
blazing through the night
the chorus chorused

Remarkable Powers. Thats stylish
the Slinger continued
while the populi have been set
to trash control, the media
dream of war, Robart dreams in transit
while he riddles the carpet on his floor

Made in Japan, the chorus chorused
Like the Zlingers Forty-four

Lets hear about your tour, I
Lil requested,

since that cold sicksties night
in Blackturkey, New Mexico, remember
when you got that cubic mile of air
pumped into your head?
We'd like to hear how ameliorating
you thought any of that stuff was

Like trying to read a newspaper
from nothing but the ink poured into your ear
First off,
the lights go out on Thought
and an increase in the thought of thought,
plausibly flooded w/ darkness,
in the shape of an ability
to hear Evil praised, takes place
then a stroll through various
corner-the-greed programs
where we encounter assorted disasters
guaranteed to secure one's comfort
After that,
an appropriate tightening down
on all the débris left over
from the Latest original question, yet

How rich with regal spoils
It was all Data Redux
caught in the ombrotrophic mire
but I sure got my Mood elevated

Like the Truth from Home, Lil agreed
Did you see the Revolution?

Well I went down to the Square
and somebody slammed a cardoor
on my Sign,
but I came thru
with certain gyroscopic effects
and despite what they say
you can see it all on the scanner
and as for Parmenides,
He's got a brain like a golfball typewriter
and really, you can feel his mind tug,
it's abstracter than a seeing eye dog

But I hear we're going out
to the big Ascension Day Burn
out at the, what is that place?

It aint no place, it's a Idea
Everything yawned, by the way
what the shuit they lobbin
inside our reduit?

That's just the man disintegrating
in this terrible heat, I replied
why don't we go outside
and join the Zlinger in the coach
I feel him signal the time to spin
and I'd like to brief him
on the Jam we're in.

The Zlinger was standing in the sunne
by the stage, his cheek reflecting
the fairness of a winter spent in Bisbee,
when the mayor's wife, a formidable lady
wearing a string of pearls
and a babyblue cardigan
came along the buckled boardwalk

He stepped smartly up to her
and said Howdy mam
and presented a large bouquet
Red Roses, expértly rendered in Solid lead

And as she felt their great weight
in her arms, a smile of regret
raced across her superbly fastidious
and disapproving lips, as she sank
slowly through the boards, out of sight

Sheer gravity, I noticed,
defined completely by its amazing inwardness

I nodded to the autocephalous horses
and said: who needs wisdom? I'm *glad*
youre not tigers!

And what I, have you brought us
from your tour of the Cumulus
the Zlinger asked

I had one eye out
for the prosecutors of Individuality
and the other eye out for the advocates
catching in that spectrum
all the known species of Cant
which I've put in this bag, here,
of fine Iranian tooling
you'll find the whole package up to date

A true gift, I, for the man
who has everything, Grammercy
That nearly completes
my speciman collection
now that I got me a real freak's lip

And then he threw it on top the coach
but, because the Zlinger undereckoned
the stupidity of dead weight
the bag flew on West
with a systematic bias toward las esquinas
some miles away, where it evidently
came to ground a few seconds later
when an oppressive nugatory roar
was heard from that quarter
and there rose up a powerful
fountain of blobs, each one consisting
of forty-two U.S. gallons of highsulphur crude

Zlinger, you better go home
Lil declared, collapsing her fan
and stepping into the coach, *somebody*
somewhere was praying for that

Well if they were in that general area
their prayers are now dripping
with hydrogen & carbon, but that thing
's as spurious as the Wortham pool

Never mind that, the Oil Smellers
have already got the scent
Everything hollered and slammed the door
and the horses reared and churned the dust
as they went quickly to the limits of Cortez
to the nightmare limits of town
through the smell of cut and bleeding grass

One thousand geodetic feet
beyond a historical marker
they came upon The Hill of Beans
in the very shadows of mesa verde
and I suggested they stop

What for, Everything asked
it don't amount to nothin

Don't give me that rock & roll,
I'm interested in the figure
not the hill I said

You mean that giant bronze bean?
that's Sllabs messenger
that memory's now obsolete

I know Everything
but I've never actually seen it
what's this inscribed
around its base?

Hecho en Tejas
para El Hughes Tool Co.

That Sllab has a lotta rind
Lil reflected opening her parasol
By the way she added *is this*
heroic or colossal
taking a coin from her purse

Neither one Everything muttered
banging on the side of Bean
with his knuckle, it's Rubber

give me that coin
we'll hear what it's got to say
Everything predicted
as the machine began to speak:

>   Achievement comes thru absolute power
>   and power comes thru strength

And Strength comes thru Digitalis
Everything screamed
cranking the finger in his ear

>   Don't overwork your lung books, son
>   your forms are not primitive enough
>   this nation is the product of reason
>   & corn
>   but that was before you were born
>   before the boiling of the seething masses
>   reduced it to commentary
>   TREMENDOUS!   FANTISTACK!

it's all over your back
like a bivouac, sorry,
I meant to say Sllab
did a fantastik job
and furthermore, left it
right in the middle of the field
at halftime, remember,
then he took a plane to the Garage
and Drove the rest of the way

Sllabs final words are thus recorded:
The Fenomena is stark, energetic
full-of-shit & well defined ═
altho there is much that I find sickening ═
the excessive opulence & waste,
the blatant commercialization
on which the society is built,
the selfish introspective approach
to world affairs, the hysterical
obsession with disease,
the puerile abhorrence of old age
& death ═ all these illnesses
are the manifestation of overdeveloped rites

   Don't look for ambiguities
    or textual tickets
   as the vocabulary blended
    in this resumé
   prohibits the use of them
     "CLICK"

Off in the vast distance
a touch of dust appeared
and a mounted group
slowly and smoothly
came into focus

And just as the poet, accompanied
by Taco Desoxin and Tonto Pronto
and our Horse arrived
there was a roar from out of town
along the road to the monument
when Dr. Flamboyant, driving
a bright green 1976 Avocado
with a white vinyl top
and full hyperbolic clutch
slid into the lot and stopped
after bouncing 25 geodetic feet
straight back off the Bean
Then he got out and squished the door shut
with his foot

Stylish, the Zlinger whispered
Thats a smart car you got there Doctor
whered you get it?

I picked it off a tree in Riverside.
Well, he then said
looking the company over
Space is rich, Time is poor
I've just been up on the mesa
preparing the reduit, we can start up
anytime. Hello Taco,

Zlinger says youre the best
environmental modification man
in the business, do you think
you can work with Portland Bill?

Well, I don know, said Taco
Yeah I think I can work with Portland Beel
if Portland Beel ever work
He's so low
he's solo
I hear he's good
at climbin trees
but I aint seen any trees
around here

I got my people down at the Corner
we straighten some fenders, by the way
that Avocado over there could use some work
and we blow some smoke stacks
burn telephone poles
slice permutationes thin as baloney
nothin complex
we also kick the perpendiculars outa right anglos
eat fur coats

suck air thru white sidewalls
but thats a Zen Act, extra
and, we do Blowtorch pretty good
we just Blowtorch Vegas from the kitchen
aprons, delante, serve the godfathers
like live spaghetti, Spaghetti con vida, activo
spend all day Holiday Inn, live spaghetti
crawl out nose, Maldición, Muy Dindán

Tres Injusto, en casa mucho madness,
Irritante! Consumidores
jump off deck Portaviones muy pronto!

We also supply Hi-grade lunatic information
you can get it here & so forth
also do Pre-pourd Scorn, that's on
twenty-four hours notice

Thats good repertoire
Dr. Flamboyant cut in,
Très chic, the Zlinger nodded
but it's not too much
to go against the Mogollones

Not the dreaded Los Mogollones!
Taco gasped with fake splendor

None Other, they are the new machinists
Masters of the wedge inclined plane screw
Silhouetted against the growing intensity
of teutonic artillery fire over the western line
Don't worry, the poet advised
a pound of gold is worth a ton of lead

Depends on what you wanta use it for
saith the horse

Just now I saw the sign
on the necklace of a crazy Zodiac
Lil announced
                    And What
did it tell you the poet asked
leafing through the Slingers
extragalactic notebook

Vegas is a vaſt *decoy*

How do you interpret it? the poet idled

A mirage it is not
It's real, like a hunter's duck

    Then we're in luck, the Horse observed
Only the duck is faithful to that deception
and when he is shot down
his temperature plunges
to meet that of his fabricated brother
Wherever *that* is
in the water of a glacial pool
in the gamebag of a metropolitan fool
or in the wagon of a suburban ghoul
Yet he may rise again when the oven's hot
to the mouth of his sporting consumer
and find his way
digested by the drafty stomach
and ignored a little later by the daffy brain
as he winds his way by porcelain bowl
to plastic pipe and concrete main
while the eye that shot him
jogs thru a page of Field & Stream
so when you multiply that bit enough
you end up in a trough of xit
and when the handle floats by you'll *pull* it!

Desperate the Poet whispered
Vicious and Desperate . . .

Men and Horses Lil smiled
share a similitude supported by foolishness
you both wear blinders
though only your race, Claude, wears them openly
I've seen them on the road
where they come and go in the same direction
and when you are made of wood I've heard
you have men in your belly
and in your arched and idealized neck
and whence from these parts they spill
to take what they could not take by storm
do you share the feast more than a fake duck?

when they take you apart
to fuel their fires and brace their hulls
and start, each one, to his disastrous home.

Uh, I'm not sure I get your question Lil
the Horse exhaled, but
are you speaking of the need for horsepower?

Yes, I suppose I am, In Horses!

How would you like poco coito, Lil?
Claude asked suddenly

My virtue is not presently on the market, fella
Lil glared, *which is bad timing of course*
because I might be amused
to make it with a horse.

Make *It*, Claude frownd
It aint nothin but a neuter pronoun.

You've got no sense of cooperation Horse,

> *Now that we stepped*
> *out of our coach,* Lil continued
> *and beneath this monument recline*
> *with our jug, can you sing*
> *an* ordinary *song*
> *after the wailing of that Firecar passes*

Hows that?
How's what?
What meanst thou?

Well, like your mother
would like to hear

Ah Yes, That Teſt
reflected the Poet through the slits
of his psychic blind . . .

Are you a relative Lil
of the famous Cocaine Lil?
The Chicago Lady   .
whose story opens with the quatrain:

> Did you ever hear about Cocaine Lil?
> She lived in Cocaine town on Cocaine hill,
> She had a cocaine dog and a cocaine cat,
> They fought all night with the cocaine rat.

Those lines are on the mirror
if she was a woman
then she is my sister!

A marvelous reflection Lil
That's when Sandberg was a𝒩 iceberg.

How about a song then
my mother sung to me when
I was small and in her arms
it is her song
but mine as I remember it,
a song of Times Paſt

Nostalgia for lunch!

I wanted you to make one up
but let us hear the one you heard
when you were just a pup

CO-KÁNG! is the way it begaine,
was a Girl from the montaine
raised on air and light
Erythralynn, painted with red clay
and dressed in leaves resembling myrtle
Erythra with a wig of roots
and she was vulgar and strong
as pure salt
and intuition came to her
like the red deer to a lick
to blow the bare words of insinuation
into human nature
the only nature to her,
because this Girl
is permanent Only in the air

Miss Americaine, was a mountain thaing
dressed in red bright calico
a long and tender radiating crystal
and like the knowledge in her nose
a lioness, intense
to the switching of the Inner Trail
which leads by hidden passage
to the Absolute Outside
yes, dressed in red bright calico
the sunne moves down
on the girl from Cuzco

Bright Erythra, the girl in calico
when the sunne comes up on Cuzco

She snaps her fingers
and they produce the numbers
never produced before, C_{19} H_{21} , then
five times more for the fugitive NO_4
five times more to lock it ON
the awful shyness of the NO_4

Now, a man is what he thinks I suppose
it matters zero what he eats
with what he blows his nose
is what he knows, ah yes, there
where the blood docks I will be
because this is My country

And then the great raptorial birds
fly like sheets across her lenses
while down the road she goes

Such is the nature of this Dope
that upon this eastward glancing slope
the leaf is grown, and it's no mysteri
how on this terrace of our globe
the limousine was born
Look, no wheels, señor
Where the Moon's leaf was forbidden
by the Royal Inca Cocalero
who first knew outerspace
covered with blood and wax
the same as you my dear
and rode along the cordillera
in a smooth chair

Nor could, my child, that which exists
be more *Here* and less *There*
The thing that can be thot
and that for the sake of which
the thot exists
is the same as the only function
and in it the Power of Reality rides
behind the oneway vision of the darkened glass
snowblind with fixity, on the Equator

   Surrounded so by Envy there appeared
at sunrise on the first of April
Suddenly as Monco Capac at the Lake Titicaca
a man in cream-colors
a funnel hanging from his brain
saying It is all one to me where I begin
For I shall come back again there
Thus spake his Highness Mescaleen

He rode out from the tilting capitol
arrayed in the plumy cinerama
of his adrenalin
and displayed by his bioluminescence
He was as fresh as you my dear
the night you sprung from my body
covered with blood and wax and
laughing out an ode to space endlessly

    Then they met. She was a bride like Añas,
remembering the reddish disk
of which we have merely Heard
the melting occurred
and which may be jamd but not disclosed
"There lives a fonne that fuckt an earthly mother."
She whispered as they passed
And she could pass the Maclagan Test
he thought, without a cloud
Save your flattery for the nickels
She smiled, and by this simple change
their passing conveyed, apparently in the flash
of the meridian arc upon her lacquered nail's
convexion, a scoop of cryſtal like a giant &

MORE than enough it is safe to say
to satisfy the whims of bobby blue bland
Plus the latterday frenzies of duane allman

    La Bella Donna was abroad. She's the one
who turned the coffeepot upsidedown in Tulsa
who maintains the madness of mumbling

She rose like a shade between them
as they turned about to reconsider
and in turning
they were so into what they could see
they couldn't see what they were out of

And in the stillness of the spells and wonders
an interruption of the indifferent flow of the sunne
rather as the scarce planets
who keep it for a while clasped in their penumbras
until the parsed rays flow from the point of the cone
they pass into futurity
and the whole system can see whats going on
in the third orbit

   My Darlings!
Doña Bella greeted them
there you are, thrilled as parallels
shining in the geometric morning

Then Doña Bella whispered
to their surprise, my principle
will prop open your disguise
This is the genuyne stuff
I keep in the veins of my vine, she said

Then cast the distillation into their eyes
and the dream came

Now let's have a look
through that brocade, Mister Deity
You'll see it more, for a while
but we'll see it Whole, forever

right through those paki threads there
in there underneath all that Red Beetle hair
Because there's not even
a quarterinch a Inca here

and as for you my Dear Girl
she said, Turning to her cousin
I can only recommend it to your brain

you know what I mean, Americaine
since even Dr. Merck lied about his werk
I'll kiss your thaing with a drop of rain
for *any word*
which drops from you nose to your mouth
without a gettin itchy
to leave the plain truth behind

So if You dont Mind, she then suggested
you can take your Big Visions, *Off my road*
and Watch out for that Toad!

Thus she had the drop on their eyes
and they were rigid along their vectors
and they saw thru each other the Correctors
with eyes that were mined in Kimberley
and cut and polished in Amsterdam . . .

thwang! thwang thwang

    thwang thwang! thwang!

La *L*ejanía. The poet whispers,
sweeping the ancient
threadbare blanket of the floor
resting at the monuments to volcanic action
to the last peñasco, desprendimiento
de tierra, ash & lava
mojones superboa, paisaje magnífico
masculino, all thats left of the plumbing
dikes, flues, the tubes of frozen magma
Rico, a thing to contemplate
Holly Holia, this is where
the earth bared herself
This is the old altar of fire
This is San Juan reaching
still sagrado and not consagrado
this was once plasta
now a worn and bitter fugue by Chaos

    This is the quantus
laid as bare as it can be laid
It doesnt do to enter it
its scale is revelátory
not comparative, it never worked
to cast the myth
too close to this place

Is that all you see?
the Horse asked in his hammock
from this our reduit

Nay, mein Pferdehändler
the poet answered
his glass in his hand

Beneath the twisted rose boughs of the heat
our shadows walk like little foreigners

Shape without form
shade without colour

Other interviewers have set
strange feet upon the set
There are some consumed
by a blinding meditation

zeveral xeiks xilly xally in the xade
enwrapped in the winding cloth
of their long-winded algebraic logic

They are going to marry those dumb ones
the ones with hands like chainsaws

This is a discreet rumor
Till quarrying starts us with amazed shock
hooked claws, wrinkled scale
This is a dragon flock
There won't be a defense of anything
All is Kaput

And now, from down at the bottom
comes the Product, Robarts Mogollones

Creeping Craters! The poet gasped
a lone caballero is galloping thru that mess
headed straight for this mesa

That would be Portland Beel
called Taco,
from under the Avocado
Hees always late, eh Tonto?

Incidentally, how you doin
with Everything's ear

Well it's like the cork & bottle
problem: I don't know whether
try to get it out
or shove it all the way in
in a way it wld have been better
if I had cut off the whole hand
at least that way we'd be presented
with a conventional sign
we'd Get the Picture, cosmetically speaking
But the way it is, with what
we've got to work with here
and what with the way that finger
keeps twitching . . . oh by the way Everything
can you feel anything
in the finger? You Can?
A ghost hand?

Zlinger, this is the most pre-classical case
I've had in 20 years of Ear Eye Nose & Throat
of the problems of the *external auditory canal*

I've seen impacted cerumen (wax to you)
boils, strictures due to blame I mean flame
bony growths, malignants, caries and necrosis
and, just plain foreign bodies
but this case has got me stumped, although
come to think of it, it's probably common
there being only one other place
where anthropos usually has his finger
but we never had a case like this in *Toronto*
by the way what's Etzalqualitzli?
it's *stamped* on this finger

Some kina corn and beans
But I can't say exactly what
the Zlinger said from under his hat

Speaking of ears, Tonto Pronto continued
did you know the length of the ears
in comparison with that of the skull
in North American Hares
varys with the temperature?

I reckon I thought it was the width
so What can you do about my receiver?

Well, from this cabaña
you can see for miles
but that don't help your ear
I could make an artificial finger
for your other ear, but . . .

Cut that xit pronto, Everything shouted

Now careful lad,
remember we aint had
our hearing impaired
I think I'll recommend
a finger specialist in Big Bend

He a friend of yours, Everything suspicioned

No, but he's the only finger specialist
I ever heard of, in the meantime
I'll give you a prescription for a ring
at least people will think you're married
to it

Now, from the north the Single Spacers
have breached the pass the Poet cast
peering through his telescope
How much optical recovery do you get
with that thing
Tonto Pronto enquired

Quite a bit Quite a bit
Dr. Flamboyant replied
manning the monitor
we can see the Octane tanks
hangin on the Mogollones side
they can't breathe the air you know
the conditions out here
are way too pure and slow

I know they brought their tanks along
I heardem all the way to *L.A.*
when they put em on

I also hear a full set of Tortillas
Double Agony Slicks, Ãkron Specials
screatch onto a siding
in downtown Pagosa Springs
And dealers are climin all over it

How you know theyre dealers
from your teeth clamped down on that knife
stickin in that tree Everything questioned

Because, Kimosabe, they're shouting
Dynamite in their dreams

That's the Home Truth, Everything reflected

Who do the Mogollones belong to Doc
Taco wanted to know

They all belong to Robart
[altho they don't necessarily know it
Theyre his version of anti-personnel
Their messenger came over in a submarine
He likesem because they got no vices
of course they got no virtues either
since those two qualities are alike
the result of natural processes
in other words these types
are totally Anti-Darwinian

Love it or Kill it, the Zlinger snorred

They are all verna, homegrown slaves

On the Other Hand
the Single Spacers are Anythingarians
Ie, opposed to nothing [that would
include Everything, at least
before his accident

They belong to anything they can get
their tongs around, theyre really
monotremata,
but they've adapted
and now most of them wear shoes
if thats the word
for such a jacked up footcover
in order to get their heads
above the crowd

Well who do we want to win
and what's next, Everythin perplexed

We don't care who wins
None of that bunch trusts us
and if they werent so careless
they'd trust us even less
but my moneys on the Mongollones
theyre gonna burn those singlespacers out

Hard to say, the poet cautioned
make no mistake, the Singlespacers
are good, in fact, theyre *Awful*
streaming in like a horde
of chromeplated ball bearings
To warm up they throw bags of bolts
into turbine generators

or tear the toenails off Bengal tigers
and just before they come on the field
they push a Black & Decker high speed drill
into the trunk of a Bull Elephant
or sometimes
they just kick a gorilla in the balls

Serious Warm-Up, Everything agreed

Yes, the Horse expanded,
I interviewed one of their number
down on the blanket
Their favorite orDœurve
is electric eels,
which they swallow alive and whole
shocking habit,
theyre the original slime mould

Where they comin from Lil called
from under the shade of a juniper tree

Theyre going to LA I said
but theyre *outa* Hardass Tennessee
and they seem to have done something
to the subduction zone
look over there at that cone
the way it's huffing and puffing

Upon hearing this news the Zlinger
lit up a Sullivan and leaned back
his eyes fixed in cryptæsthesic isolation
His mind hung bat-like
from the rafters of the Burlington Arcade

He rolled the seed ball
of a *platanus occidentalis*
in his finger, his minde
played over the austenitic horizon
and gaged the coefficient of expansion
The immense inertia of the old order
buckles that chain of blue mountains
This is old dinosaur country
a record full of sudden changes

I see the grass shake in the sunne
for leagues on either side the chorus sung
Oh Zlinger are we lost

No, we are crystals of gold
along the axes of upheaval
When, he asked, will they
take up all their tappet clearance

Round Lunchtime, the Doctor theorized

The amateurs trouble, the Zlinger pondered
is over-revving, quite often
with a cold engine, and that would lead
he knew, to inertial failures of the Big End
fatigue cracks, the separation of the Bosses
from the Crown
This will be very low-grade glory
this cranking up for the chiliad
he said

At this very moment
a zephyr struck the mimosa

as down the draw / and up the hill
rode the very intrepid / Portland Bill

That's a grotesque exercise
you got down there
he addressed the Zlinger
who was still suspended
in his mental hanger
we the only spectators here?

It's a Big-Ticket Item
the Horse responded

Vaz This, Portland Bill blurted
from behind his moustache
a Shpeaking Horse?

Shuks, the Horse laughed
and kicked a barrel labeled crackers
You think Thats inconvenient
listen to my Friend here
The Speaking Barrel

Can he *walk*? No, but he can roll
He hangs out with the tumbleweeds
and he loves to talk

I can believe that Everything noticed
look at the way it vibrates
You better ask it a question
before it busts a band
Hokay, Portland Bill blurted
What about Oil
I aint no drum! the Barrel shouted

No No! Portland Bill exploded
I mean Rangoon Tar

UhHuh! you'll settle for anything
On the other hand,
the Barrel began to expand
They can now grow Reindeer Commercially,
Rather unsettling news for Reindeer
And I heard
they've crossed the feeble & the bold
Rather unsettling news for Feebalo
They say depressions
are nearly always due to chemical imbalance
But the only cure they can think of is Taalk
But the best bet of all,
would be to choose
an impeccable gem from the new snobbery:
Don't give your drippy offspring
an electric train for christmas
Givem a Railroad!
In other words, fancy face
if you can't improve your standard
improve your mind
and remember, autoinsurance companies
really take the public for a ride

And Now
          How'd Yawl lika riddle

Oh speak Barrel
The chorus *shook*

Well, you know the trouble with D.C.
theyre all coked out to their ears
have been for years
And you know the trouble with S.F.
can't get enough
of that wonderful stuff
And you know the trouble with Chi
still singin
pie in the sky
And you know the route to L.A.
It's about two inches deep!
And you know the trouble with Lanta
they just do what they gotta
So where does that leave NY?
Here's soot in your eye!

Practical to the last detail,
Everything remarked
But has that got something to do
with the News
Everything scratched his head

When you snooz you looz, the Barrel said

Yes, but that can cut two ways
Everything protested
It can for a while
the Barrel observed
you know more about crackers
than I do!

Now I didnt bring them up
Everything disallowed,
Somebody here's
making a pitch to the crowd

The condition of your stomach
is personal to you
the Barrel interrupted
I'm speaking from the standpoint
of an Object
and I get more sure of myself
as I settle in

What about the riddle
Everything enquired
what kind of answer have you got
after all, youre just a barrel of crackers

Well, I have, uhhuum
the Barrel began to extol
looked at the bottoms
of a lot of feet
and Never saw a sole

But the system works!
Everything quoted
or have you got another version
of how we got here?
The WHAT works! The WORKS work,
you fancy faced digit!
What's that finger doing in your ear?
churned the Barrel

Now you better hold your staves
Everything threatened
or I'm liable to unwrap you

I wouldn't try that Hothead
this contraption youre talking to
might spring apart in your, uh face
continued the Barrel indifferent to caution
Anyway Everything I *do*
and It's not some Kleenex-out-the-hatch-
infection theory neither

I heard it was a can of Pork & Beans
over the rail
Everything chimed

No, that's too natural
grinned the Barrel
It's all over your meat
and what you eat
for instance there's this citizen
is out looking for produce
He's got a little on his lapel
Nothing specific,
could be anything from chinese
to italian
by the way
you might be interested
to know whats going on in this church
Up in Seattle (where I caught rain last month
the barrel parenthesized
They call themselves the Pulpers

I'd sure be interested
in any church a barrel attended
Everything prodded, What's it about

Strict Fidelity!
They allow *Nothing*

Oh, you mean no sing no dance
All work no play? Everything gaped

Not quite. They start before that,
No Breathe

Plain Jesus! is that a fact

Not yet, theyre in the slogan stage
Theyve cranked consumption down
to plain water, that was my job
till I got pneumonia
and went back to crackers
But theyre bracing for the Boreal Invasion
bury their dead and not quite dead
in the roots of trees
some consign their money
directly to the ice

That's nice, Everything waited

They belong to the Scare Story Chapter
a subgroup
and some plan to leave
all they can think of to a dawg

I can see what you mean
by Strickt Fidelity Everything marveled
that's pure Egyptian

Yes, the signs are all over the sidewalk
the Barrel resonated
it's the new Freedom

Now I don't know what you mean
by freedom, Barrel
But you better keep your lid on
or you might get used for pickles
Do not deny in the new vanity
the old, original dust

You can't scare me Everything
because I aint a pickle barrel

That's your distinction
it dont mean a thing to us
because when we get in a lot of pickles
we throwem in the first barrel we see!
And that aint the worst of it
When the Mogollones get here
Theyre liable to fit your case
on a single pickle
and marry you off to a gate post
where youll take delivery on the mail
until some drunk
comin home late at night
in a camaro jacked up with flames
devours you!

Ho Ho the barrel puffed
I'm gonna be saved by the Nature Lobby
I'm very well crafted you know
authentic Old Time
and I still got my lid
it's around here someplace

I wouldnt count on the nature lobby Barrel
Portland Bill said
stickin his hand in for a cracker
looks like theyre not gonna show up

Get your hand outa me!
the barrel rumbled, I know you
youre a sponger of exemplary singlemindedness
and absolutely no astuteness
besides, one cracker leads to another
and I aint no pork-barrel neither!

What's it like down there on the flat
Bill, the poet asked

It's like Brutalidad, quarks
zippin right out of the main manifold
it's the tamale finale
screamin zucchini impaled on pinnacles
all the hysteria of a fake disaster set
I was able to talk briefly with Trig Utah
the matinée idol of the Mogollones
who travels on a diesel-powered skateboard
holding a hatful of dinosaur piss
and he said Robart was shipping them a
full carload of peste bubónica
real over the border quality

but then somebody fucked really strong
with the subduction zone and I saw
this fixed head coupe clear the horizon
doing a full charge ton and that's
when I skedaddled

Here, I've got it
I'm almost inside, the doctor cried
but that car has got so much lead
around it
       May I present
       sputtered thru the monitor
       His Holinas the 19th Hodunkas
       of Hot Springs

       Krackle Krackle Krackle

       Incarnation is bunk, Al
       Get that Punk outa here
       And send for the Hydralicx
       we're in a fracture
       surprise is no longer the mode
       We gotta get as big as we can
       as fast as we can, that's the game plan

       Can't do that Patrón
       He don't pray for rain no more
       he was a happy man
       but they kicked him upstairs
       and moved him to Chicago

       He travels fastest who travels alone
       ¡Adiós!

Robart shouted as the side
of the Chester White Special
Came down on pulleys
and he spurrd down the gangplank on his cow,
not exactly an ordinary cow,
white hands clinging to the tightened rein
and ran straight for the border

That's a long way
if he's goin to Chile
Everything observed

But that's no hoss
the Doctor said, look
at the screen,
it's a naked singularity
he must be headed for Siberia!

Off in the distance there
the Poet pointed
are those guys workin on the railroad

Sí señore, Taco squinted
theyre choppin down the watertower

Wellwellwell, the doctor raved
it looks like the Magma Source was saved

Lil patted the Zlingers cheek
and asked him if he could speak
*Looks like you slept
thru most of that* she said

But you'll be happy to learn
that Robart's redshifted again
and all the Atlantes
tumbled out of the car
and made for the skislopes
we've effected the saneamento!

So Robart didn't carry out
his purge of the Atlantes
while passing thru Iowa
as threatened. That's
welcome news Lil
Oh, hello Bill, the Zlinger blinked.

Get your dog away from me
the Barrel rumbled
I can't stand that thing, it's mental!

You don't like my dog? asked Bill
No, get it outa here
it's a hunk of trash on four legs!

Why you crazy crackerbarrel
Bill sputtered and drew a Big Revolver
I'm gonna make you look
like a hunk of gruyère

I think I'm gonna retch Lil said

Not around me the barrel rolled
And just as it reached
the lip of the mesa
it stalled, stuck against a clod

Wrong Way, the Zlinger called
and then the earth shook
and the barrel rolled over
and the finger fell out of Everything's ear
and in the distance he could hear
a vast rheumatism

Many the wonders this day I have seen
the Zlinger addressed his friends
Keen, fitful gusts are whispering here and there
The mesas quiver above the withdrawing sunne
Among the bushes half leafless and dry
The smallest things now have their time
The stars look very cold about the sky
And I have grown to love your local star
But now niños, it is time for me to go inside
I must catch the timetrain
The parabolas are in sympathy
But it grieves me in some slight way
because this has been such fine play
and I'll miss this marvellous accidentalism

Oh no, Zlinger, Lil trembled
*must you leave now, we've just hit the Top
and you belong to us*

Ah Dear Lillian, give me a kiss
you *know* my heart beats to another radio signal

Whats it like, Lil asked

Our Source is self refracting
and when it rises it actually plays a tune
on one's eyeballs, Maximum Deum
and our birds have two heads and sing duets

Holy xit, Everything wept

and the cows have the ability
to convert their teets
in the summertime
when they give a substance
not unlike tasty-freeze

Rather convenient said the Horse
who was speaking on the phone
to Frank Chrystler Canlid, the great producer

Yes, since the trees
bear a double cone
Where then, Lily are you off to?
as this company scatters on the marvellous winde

I have this incomparable feeling
and it keeps calling me home
a feeling of Wyoming
I'd like to get back,
before they tear off the dome

And you Poet,
whats in the cards for you

Moving to Montana soon
going to be a nose spray tycoon

Give my regards to Portland
Sure will said Bill

Good work doctor
shows what you can do
if you persevere
Do you mind if I keep your hand
as a souvenir

Goodbye I, keep your eye
on the local species
theyre nothing but
a warehouse full of peanuts

But how will you get there
the poet asked

I'll go along with the tachyon showers
which are by definition faster than light
& faster than prime
I'll be home by suppertime

Adiós Taco
Goodbye Tonto
and take my greetings
to the lads in Toronto
Goodbye to Everything
waved the Zlinger thru the dust veil

Vaya con ojo caliente
vaya con zapatas, muchachos
vaya con mucho infinito y voluptuoso
Adió por eternidad, Lindas
Hasta la Vista!

Linotype: Caslon Old Face & Caslon No. 137
Bodoni Book, Granjon, Remington. Foun
dry: Calson 471, Bauer Bodoni, Ultra
Bodoni, Bodoni Bold, Garamond, Co
mstock: Spring Creek San Franci
sco. Printer's Button and Lady
Caslon G by M. Myers. Spec
ial effects by H. Teter. Text
from Wivenhoe, Lawren
ce, Taos, Ardleigh, Ch
icago, Cuernavaca, K
ent, Riverside, Lo
ndon, Kimmerid
ge, Wivenhoe
Park, and
Cambr
idg
e